LEARNING TO LOVE OUT LOUD

...Don't Limit Your Life to Whispers

*Inspirational Poems and Fictional Short Stories
based on truths and a study of spiritual rebirthing*

SANDRA DUKES

Editor: Donna L. Ferrier
Proofreader: Carol Freeman Porter (first proof)

Interior & Cover Layout & Design:
Tarsha L. Campbell

Published by:
DOMINIONHOUSE
Publishing & Design, LLC
P.O. Box 681938
Orlando, Florida 32868
407.703.4800 phone
www.mydominionhouse.com
****

The Lord gave the Word: great was the company of those who published it. (Psalms 68:11)

"Love not the world, neither the things that are in the world. If any man loves the world, the love of the Father is not in him. For all that is in the world, the lust of the flesh, and the lust of the eyes, and the pride of life, is not of the Father, but is of the world. And the world passeth away, and the lust thereof: but he that doeth the will of God abideth for ever."

--1 John 2:15-17 (KJV)

"A merry heart doeth good like a medicine:
but a broken spirit drieth the bones."

--Proverbs 17:22 (KJV)

DEDICATION

This book is dedicated to Our Heavenly Father and to my mother, Annie, and is written in appreciation to those who love out loud.

Special thanks to Tarsha Campbell and Mr. Washington for their unwavering encouragement. God bless you.

Throughout this book I have included Bible scriptures in honor of God's life-giving Word, along with quotes and lyrics from writers who have stimulated my mind, aroused my soul, and awakened my spirit. These writings gave me courage when there was none to be found, hope when all seemed hopeless, and laughter in spite of my wounded womb. I do this as an acknowledgment of my admiration for these anointed works and in honor and gratitude of God's creativity shining forth in the form of a writer's pen.

I have discovered that inspiration has neither age nor social boundaries and can be manifested in either the simplest act of kindness or the greatest accomplishment. It is merely the stimulation of the spirit. Along my journey, my poetry of life has found new meaning, crossing racial, gender, and chronological lines.

I have also learned that inspiration is an infinite power. It is the stimulation of the spirit brought forth when one realizes the things that cause chaos in our lives do not define us. Only by God, His plan, and our obedience to Him are we revealed and resurrected in the fullness of His glory. We have the choice to live in generational blessings or generational curses. We all have a seed planted deep inside us—a gift, a Godly pre-destined purpose; that seed can only be cultivated and bloom when we share that treasure with others."

-- Sandra Dukes

***

"When a man starts to build a world, He starts first with himself"

-- Langston Hughes, "Freedom's Plow"

TABLE OF CONTENTS

TABLE OF CONTENTS

"And be not conformed to this world: but be ye transformed by
the renewing of your mind, that ye may prove what is that good, and acceptable, and perfect, will of
God."

-- Romans 12:2 (KJV)

"Learn To Love Out Loud"

Anoint thyself and smear yourself with the Word.

For the sundown of the last and the dawn of a new first has begun.

There is newness in the air, a freshness of a newer spring, A Revival.

SPEAK TO IT! MARCH TO IT!

A Revival Speaks!

March to Your Destiny -- See Your Destiny...SPEAK TO IT! MARCH TO IT!

"Learn to Love out Loud! Don't limit your life to whispers!"

There is no agony like bearing an untold story inside you."
-- Zora Neale Hurston

What is Loving Out Loud?

Loving out loud is the conscious practice of joyful living; unscathed by disappointments, problems and hurts; unashamed of living by the Gospel of Jesus Christ. Loving out loud is having a Godly mindset, a compassionate heart full of forgiveness and understanding. It is living a life based on the Word of God and the teachings of Jesus Christ with faith and cheerful expectancy, knowing each day is full of God's promise of new mercies, new blessings, and new grace.

A New Start

When I was young I wanted fame. Later in life, I wanted fortune. Now that I am older and wiser, I know true wealth and the mark of respect are the results of fulfillment, of knowing I have made a positive difference. Life is a journey like the seasons. Youth is spring; all is new, full of curiosities and wonder. It is a time of nurturing and establishing values. Summer is full of energy, actions, and reactions. Fall is the season of solutions and resolutions, of reaping what we have sown. In the winter the ground is covered with snow and nature seems to be dismal, but underneath the dead foliage, a tiny spark of life is waiting to emerge, waiting for spring--a new start!

What Happens When We Love Out Loud?

When we learn to love out loud, a beautiful transformation occurs like the metamorphosis of a butterfly, pollinating the splendor of God's beauty to all we touch. When we learn to love out loud, we not only articulate the words of God, but we also obey the words of Jesus. When we learn to love out loud, we love one another as ourselves, embodying true Christian love. When we learn to love out loud, we become cheerleaders for a better world.

"Every book is a quotation; and every house is a quotation out of all forests, and mines, and stone quarries; and every man is a quotation from all his ancestors."

-- *Ralph Waldo Emerson*

***

"And the world will be better for this that one man scorned and covered with scars still strove with his last ounce of courage to reach the unreachable star."

- *Impossible Dream (The Quest), Lyrics by Joe Darion and Composed by Mitch Leigh*

***

"If one advances confidently in the direction of his dreams, and endeavors to live the life which he has imagined, he will meet with a success unexpected in common hours. He will put some things behind, will pass an invisible boundary; new, universal, and more liberal laws will begin to establish themselves around and within him; or the old laws be expanded, and interpreted in his favor in a more liberal sense, and he will live with the license of a higher order of beings."

-- *Henry David Thoreau, Where I Lived, and What I Lived For*

***

"God's Word nurtured His creative seed in me, which took root and flourished. By this means, the Word in me has become the God in me. God bless you, with love."

-- *Author Sandra Dukes*

CHAPTER I

CHEERLEADER REVIVAL

"Look not every man on his own things, but every man also on the things of others."
                                                                    -- Philippians 2:4

What are Cheerleaders for a Better World?

Cheerleaders for a better world (CWs) are people who choose to position themselves on the sidelines of anyone they meet to teach, pray for, and cheer on those striving to reach their goals. They say things like, "Don't give up now! You're almost there! You can do this! Look to the hills which cometh your help!"[1] They are not of the world, but for a better world, cheering on everyone they meet with their good deeds and works toward mankind. Somewhere on their found path of life they discovered a way to guard and protect the innocence of a child, to believe in and expect the best of each person they meet. They love humbly, as Matthew 18:4 says: "Whosoever therefore shall humble himself as this little child, the same is greatest in the kingdom of heaven."

CWs are people from all walks of life, "the haves" as well as "the have nots," who exhibit the love and caring necessary for inspiring others to fulfill their God-given destinies. Because they cherish Biblically based Christian love, hope, and sharing, the CW "haves" have not let their names, titles, or social positions earn or disprove the respect and honor they rightly deserve. Instead, they know "there but the grace of God go I." And the CW "have nots" harbor no resentment for their lowly position, and dutifully praise God each day for everything He gave them. They find strength and faith in the old adage, "I was sad because I had no shoes, but then I met a man with no feet."[2] So, whatever their economic or social status, CWs participate in the joy of giving and share their lives each day with those they encounter.

God finds favor in us when we show mercies to those in pain. We receive true approval when we share whatever we are blessed to offer to people in need. I am thankful for those of such character and I give God all the glory for sending CWs to surround me.

---

[1] Psalm 121.

[2] Based on poetry from the Gulistan (or "Rose Garden") of Sa'di.

LEARNING TO LOVE OUT LOUD

When I returned to college, I struggled for many years to graduate. The reason I finally did was because along that uphill climb I was pushed, pulled, and cheered on by family, friends, and strangers. Some of those strangers have now become friends.

A Tribute to Cheerleaders for a Better World

Encouragement is spiritual medicine that is as imperative to one's health as medicine is for an ailing body. A word of support can heal the disheartened spirit. When I became physically ill, Dr. Macbeath; his nurse, Amber; and the rest of his staff came to my rescue time after time. There are no words to express my appreciation for their medical treatment, concern, and love.

Over the years, I've also received support and encouragement from many teachers and mentors with CW spirits, such as Professor Douglas Hoppock, who I affectionately call "Papa," even though I am his senior; Angel Ward, a cute, petite young woman with a cheerleader's smile, who diligently tutors and encourages struggling math students after her classes; along with Dr. Doris Davis, Professor of English; Dr. Glenda Ballard and Dr. Gaynell Green of the Bachelor of Applied Arts and Sciences program; Casey Roberts, TV Productions Instructor in the Texas A&M Media Services Department; Administrative Assistant Connie Brian, an angel at Texarkana College; and retired Del Mar College Professor Dorothy Benson-Brown, who has been an unwavering mentor to so many for more than fifty years and my creative arts muse since I was a young woman.

From my earliest beginnings, I have been inspired by teachers such as Mrs. Trimble, the first person who taught me why education was so vital (especially as a black woman in those times) to achieve any hopes and dreams of a better life. I have also been blessed by other teachers of the academic world, such as my friends Geraline (Gerri) Hart-Ray and Ms. Maudie Watson. I honor the teachers of today who continue to teach with the same giving heart and spirit as Mrs. Trimble. Teachers with such character dedicate their lives to our children each day.

They have accepted a lifelong challenge to unlock young minds to do better, live better, and be better, and I have been blessed to have been influenced by so many. Professor Randy Nobles, who has now departed this life, was a wonderful and brilliant man who possessed a meek and humble heart and spirit despite his impressive background. He taught me that sometimes we have to take slow, steady steps in order to accomplish large, hard, and long tasks, as if we were "eating an elephant one spoonful at a time."

I am inspired by the skilled messengers of the Gospel, who teach each day by living according to the holy Word. I am also inspired by the "Mosaic Generals" who don't necessarily have a minister's license or pulpit to teach or preach from but preach the Gospel anyway. They sit on front porches every day and witness about Jesus' love and salvation to anyone who passes by.

Whether CWs are family, friends, or strangers, I give God my thanksgiving for these unselfish souls who cheer others on to achieving their Godly purpose. These are people who, in spite of others' failures or faults, and in the midst of their own troubles and heartaches, reach out to assist, asking nothing in return except for those they help to learn, live, love, and share. People who share their lives, struggles, and testimonies to inspire others are the truest CWs. I admire them because of their accomplishments and their compassion for their fellow man. I honor them because of their hearts. Whether they are world renowned or only succeed in common, everyday goals, who they are is still an inspiration to all. As the wise old saying goes, "Some people are like flowers. Their beauty is in just being."

Each of us should leave the legacy we were freely given in John 13:34; learn and live according to Ephesians 4:32 ("Instead be kind to one another…"); strive for a world that lives according to Romans 12:9-13 ("Don't just pretend to love others, really love them. Hate what is wrong. Hold tightly to what is good") and Matthew 5:44 ("But I say to you…"); teach 1 Peter 4:8 ("Above all, love each other deeply"); show evidence that love prospers, as written in Proverbs 17:9; and abide in faith, hope, and love, while remembering the greatest of these is love, according to 1 Corinthians 13:13. These are the laudable, unselfish acts of charity attributed to creating a better world. Learning to love out loud is the beginning of birthing cheerleaders for a better world and achieving a sacrosanct (holy, sacred, inviolable) deliverance.

"I am inspired that we each are a universe within a universe,
a tiny speck of God out of God."
                                              -- *Author Sandra Dukes*

"A Tribute to Cheerleaders for a Better World"
Inspiration Revisited in Cryptic Prose

Stanza 1[3]
Inspiration is received as simply as learning the "A B Cs"
An alphabetical puzzle deciphered the riddle
of Pharaoh's hieroglyphics it has traveled
Borne of the Hebrew slaves' hope trudged on
Twenty-six fierce Roman soldiers marching across 500,000 continents
Conquering pictures, words, and stories
Grecian artisans warring against the jailers of ignorance
A Democratic form grasping for freedom
Releasing syntactic speakers into a phonetic world
The Alpha and the Omega[4]
In the beginning[5] was the word and the word was with God
And the Word was God
Inspire me
Inspire me to be

Stanza 2[6]
Nearly three decades have I journeyed to return to this place
Where I wandered long ago only to return and face
That life is more than living and living is less than being alive
That what inspired me in my youth has transpired and thrived
That the feeling that once shook my soul and brought me to joyful tears
has crossed genders races and chronological years
That what once was, still is, and what is has been encrypted
Replacing foolishness for wisdom, grandeur for grace
A seeking of the Spirit via joy and pain, laughter and tears
Restoring the birthright of faith out of the transgressions of fears

Stanza 3[7]
With the passing of the old, the reclaiming of the new
My adage has been reformulated my observation proved untrue
My theory life brought heartbreak my hypothesis to hide
Life had become a place I visited never to reside
The theory failed in merit a contradiction wrought
For an extroverted recluse is formed from the bowels of a coward's thoughts
For joy is simply allowed when we entwine
Our ecstasies our agonies, our failures our faults
The vow of life we have persistently sought

---

[3] The history of the alphabets and the forming words.
[4] The beginning and the end--God.
[5] John 1:1
[6] The author's personal journey and testimony.
[7] The author's personal journey and testimony, continued.

Stanza 4

In seeking I found my answer and it was akin
With *Pilgrims*[8], pioneers, and farmers since time began
You cannot sow a seed on parched and barren land
The substance of the quest is in the essence of the man

Stanza 5

Crusading across fields of danger
Reaching mountains of pleasure
A theatrical plan delivered[9]
to a campaign of invention my transformation began
Mounted on vast and hallowed lands
Where *Noble*[10] men and women, descendants of authority do sit
Caretakers of the beacon upon which historical futures shine
Lighters of the lanterns, keepers of the minds
Rocking chaired rulers, wizards of rhymes
(Riddle) "How does one eat an elephant?"
(Answer) "One spoonful at a time"

Stanza 6

Inspired by this wisdom led by the beacon's light
A journey of victory came within sight
A dominion among twin cities of *Green*
where scholars echo a ballad (*Ballard*) of wit[11]
To someday be our privileged
To somehow grasp the gist
To some way bear the burden
Where Cheerleading authority sits
Inspire me Inspire me to be

---

[8]Bo Pilgrim, co-founder and senior chairman of Pilgrim's Pride, benefactor of community college scholarships.

[9]North East Texas Community College, nestled between Dangerfield, Mt. Pleasant, and Pittsburg, Texas. Excellent theatre-arts program headed by Professor Douglas "Papa" Hoppock.

[10]Professor Randy Nobles.

[11]The BAAS program at Texas A&M--Texarkana. Dr. Gaynelle Green is the head of the program, and Dr. Glenda Ballard is the Dean of the College of Education and Liberal Arts.

Stanza 7[12]
I am inspired that we each are a universe within a universe
Tiny specks of God out of God
By the might of the pen the slayer is slain
A lesson of a proverbial wisdom
A lesson of a philosophical claim
God is my Author He knows me by name
This Tedious Journey I traveled crossing my Red Seas[13]
My testimony is that my *Lord Jesu*s carried me

Stanza 8
UN harnessed mules, vacant bird cages
Cultivated roots in my mother's gardens
and the purple hues at the ends of rainbows
Inspire me
The Bible, Zora Langston Angelou, Alice Walker, Alex Haley, Gwendolyn Truman, Judith Ortiz Cofer,
Doris Davis[14]*, Jorge Luis Borges, and J. California Cooper*[15]
Inspire me
Literary Evangelism,
that prophetically hears and speaks
"Beyond the Open Mic"
"Battered Clergy"
Rising out of their ashes
Teaching and Preaching in spite of…

---

[12] Praise to God, the Creator.

[13] Anointed Works, a theatre ministry founded and play written by Sandra Dukes.

[14]Author Doris Davis, Professor of English at Texas A&M University--Texarkana.

[15]Noted poets and authors.

Anointed Apostolic Authors

The Theresa H. Johnsons
Joseph B. Howards
Inspire me Inspire me to be

Bishop T.D. Jakes
Declaring and Decreeing "Woman Thou Art Loosed"
Inspired the God--created me
To Be

I am inspired
that deep within the poetry's womb grows words ideas ideals nurtured from the
umbilical blood of God and nourished by the breast milk of mankind
Inspiring dreams stories lyrics and rhymes
Laying pulsating growing waiting
Until its season until its time
Floating dancing kicking tearing fighting through the passage of birth
To be seen to be heard

Stanza 9
I am inspired by *Shakespearian* physicians
under an *Amber* light[16]
Constant hope gatekeepers
standing watch among the stacks[17]
bestowing inner sight

I am inspired by the sent blessings
Of teachers who became *"Papas"*[18]
Uncles that became brothers
Brothers becoming God-sent men
Friends that became sisters
Sisters that became friends

---

[16]Dr. Blair Macbeath, nurse Amber, and staff.

[17]Connie Brian, Information Resources Assistant and Library Staff at Texas A&M and Texarkana College Libraries.

[18]Professor Douglas Hoppock, head of the theatre-arts program at North East Texas Community College, nestled between Dangerfield, Mt. Pleasant, and Pittsburg, Texas.

I am inspired by
The strength of a Godson once caged now set free
Breaking the curses and claiming a father's dignity
You--inspire me to be

I am inspired by transformations
From generational curses into generational blessings
The cleansing of this dirty rag
Wring out of the crevices and altars of new mornings and the dusking of the past
Of aged Vikings unashamed bearing scars of valor, wash pot tithing with a plan.
Of maids to mentors, broken wing doves becoming soaring eagles
Of the secular hurts
Betrayals anguish bitterness hate
discarded on a liberating trash day

I am inspired by the letter O and its strength[19]
The Obamas Osteens Oprahs
The Overcomers and the Overseers

I am inspired by the letter O transformations
Its strength its circular continuous power
From letter to word to explanation to exclamation beyond exaltation
"O' Lord" a double calling of His Name
From natural man beyond carnal man towards the spiritual man
The transformation of the proverbial village and child to a proverbial world and people
"Forever O' LORD, Your Word is settled in heaven"

Stanza 10
"Mine eyes have seen" the blight of destruction,[20]
Only to witness hope[21] take breath and rise again
The lifting of the iron curtain the falling of the wall the burning of twin towers the answering
of the heroes' call

---

[19]"O" is actually a double calling on the name of the Lord because it's both a word and a letter that means circular, continuous, and neverending. "O" is an exultation, an explanation, and an exclamation. Ex. Psalm 119:89, "Forever, O LORD, your word is settled in heaven."

[20]Wars.

[21]Freedom and justice, such as lifting the iron curtain, removing the physical barrier between Eastern and Western Europe.

"O, say can you see by the dawn's early light
...from Sea to shining sea"
that within us the Maker has provided ...all we truly need to be
Martin, Malcolm, Mandela, the Kennedys, Bunche, Young, Judges Thurgood Marshall,
Mathis, Lopez, Joe Brown

Inspire me

I am inspired by words budding from "I have finally been included in"
"We, the people" Pollinating into "Yes We Can!"[22]
Life, liberty, and the pursuit of happiness inspires me

Patricia Harris, Madeleine Albright, Condoleezza Rice, Judges Sharon Pratt,
Hatchett, Mabelean, Toler, Cristina

Inspire me to be

...And the roll call goes on

So "why should I be discouraged" at the injustice of Jena 6
When God's eye has kept the sparrow there is nothing He can't fix
"In the beginning there was darkness...and God said let there be light."[23]
Therefore, my inspiration of goodness is never far from God's sight

Stanza 11
I am inspired by the spectrum colors at the end of the rainbow

The Constant courage of the color Pink--faith racing to a cure[24]
Walker's "The Color Purple"--exploding and exposing the never asked--the never said
Jimmy Hendrix's psychedelic sound of a purple hazed "America"
Ray Charles' "for spacious skies of " Blues
I am inspired by America the Beautiful
me being me
And you being you

---

[22] 44th President of the United States of America Barack Obama.

[23] Genesis 1:1

[24] Honoring those who lost the race against breast cancer, the survivors and their families; and to the many dedicated teams and participants in the "race to a cure" throughout the United States.

Stanza 12
"Who I am is not a reflection of you but who I have become."[25]
"From *The Dorothea Towles*[26] stomping runways to the *Banks*
Ripping to shreds the beauty myth
Inspire me to be me

I am inspired by designers and fashionistas
Friends who taught me to catwalk the walk and to talk that talk
Friends with Candied Adam's apples--"Thanks Wong Foo"
A movie that took the Boo! Out of taboo

I am inspired by
Elizabeth "Bessie" Coleman[27] *and Ruth Carol Taylor*[28] who led the way Pinned with metal
wings we flew into a new dawning into a new day

I am inspired by
the Mitchells, the Jamisons, the Aileys
The knitting of limbs into wings
Expressions in movement depicting theatrical scenes
I am inspired by those who dare
Thespians floating on the Butterfly's wing
The Hatties,[29] *the Bo jangles*[30], *the Dandridges, the Winfreys, the Berrys, the Perrys*
Travailing in-flight
No matter the obstacles they dare to dream they dare to act they dare to write
continuing the tradition of resisting of what was unheard
Birthing reality to what was considered "utterly absurd"

I am inspired by
A grandfather's legacy, a father's impartation, a praying mother's determination,
a family's devout dedication, a child's plea, a wife's wailing, and a husband's moan

I am inspired by God's Anointed
From small hamlets to the metropolitan
Dusty country roads Street corner sanctuaries Storefront stands Cathedral pulpits

---

[25]Giving glory to God, my Creator, and giving thanksgiving for the CWs, which include my family.

[26]Dorothea Towles Church, the first successful black model in Paris.

[27]The first African-American woman to earn a pilot's license.

[28]The first African-American airline stewardess (flight attendant) in the United States.

[29]Actresses Hattie McDaniel and Thelma Butterfly McQueen, the first black Americans to win Oscars, both in Gone with the Wind.

[30]Actor and dancer, Bill "Bo jangles" Robinson.

Praying generals sitting on Mosaic *(Mozelle)*[31] front porches who warred for my soul
The Patrick Lloyds--Alonzo Greens--Robert Canadys--Hagees--Dollars--Jonas Clarks--Dukes--
Fannie Madison Wallaces--Cindy Trimms--Joyce Meyers--Juanita Bynums and the Linda
Morables--Sheryl Bradys--Jakes of this world binding and loosening
what is in heaven here on earth in Jesus' Name.
"For once I was blind, but now I see"

I am inspired by *Anne Wright's* "Battle for your Seed"
And the roll call of "The Called" goes on and on...[32]

I am inspired by "I AM that I AM"[33]
The Old Testament and The New
The Book of 66 books
The partaking of its writing
Spanning sixteen hundred years
A book that gives joy; not ashes, not tears
I am inspired by ministers that live by these words
(Ephesians 4[34] and Ephesians 3[35])
For words need to be seen, not just spoken, not just heard

Who I am is not a reflection of you but who I have become
"A universal blessing given to all a global share
Because of you I believe
Because of you I dare
And the roll call goes on...Inspire me Inspire me to be

---

[31]Mozelle Parnell

[32]Isaiah 61:1-3

[33]"And God said unto Moses, I AM THAT I AM..." (Exodus 3:14)

[34]Walk in unity.

[35]The mystery revealed.

"Now faith is the substance of things hoped for,
The evidence of things not yet seen."[36]
The pride given to my heritage for all that it is
I embrace and pay tribute:
From slaves and servants to wash gals and yard boys
the well of faith sprang
Forging the way through illiteracy
Stumbling falling sometimes crawling

Readers of the Word and the academic world
Maids to cosmetologists
preachers teachers and nurses
bus porters to the Pentagon
privates to captains and commanders
The Begat and the Begotten
The uncovering of the wells[37]
Inspire me
Inspire me to be

Who I am is not a reflection of you
but who I have become
And you
Inspire me
Inspire me to be

And the roll call goes on

And on and on………..And On!

---

[36]Hebrews 11:1

[37]Isaiah 12:3 and John 4:4-14

"Show me your hands. Do they have scars from giving? Show me your feet. Are they wounded in service? Show me your heart. Have you left a place for divine love?"

---*Fulton J. Sheen*

CHAPTER II

LEARNING TO LOVE OUT LOUD

"And this is our confidence, that if we pray according to His will, He will hear us, and give us what we ask for, because our desires are in agreement with His thoughts for us."

--1 John 5:14-15

Chapters 2 and 3 contain short stories and poems based on truths, some of which have been enhanced with fiction of my own, or observing others' personal experiences, that address the human desire and need to love and be loved. In seeking to possess this great gift of love, however, we sometimes fall short of enjoying the Biblical love that 1 Corinthians 13: 1-13 teaches.

The Bible contains many examples of love between a man and a woman: Adam and Eve, Abraham and Sarah, Isaac and Rebekah, Boaz and Ruth, Joseph and Mary, Jacob and Rachel, David and Bathsheba, Samson and Delilah, along with the chronicles of Ahab and Jezebel and Ananias and Sapphira. The Lord taught all of these famous (or infamous) couples the blessings that come with obeying His Word, and warned them of the curses and tragedies that would befall them if they disobeyed. This is why we need to learn, experience, and express what Biblical love is.

Love is the deep-seeded foundation of our lives. Our five senses (seeing, hearing, smelling, tasting, and touching) are captives to love. We express love in the way we adorn and perfume ourselves; in our need to touch and be touched; the loving preparation of a meal and the words we write, speak, and sing. But there is no greater expression of love than the love of God. "Stone Love" by Brent Jones and TP Mobb, recorded in 2007 on *The Ultimate Weekend* CD, epitomizes the love relationship God has with us as His children. We all need and seek love, but when we give up on ourselves, Jesus, our Rock, the one who never leaves us nor forsakes us, loves us beyond our faults. He says, "I love you; you're beautifully and wonderfully made," and that's what "Stone Love" is all about.

So, what does love have to do with it? Everything, my beloveds--everything!

"Old Vikings Bear Scars"

She was running like she had never run before; running to quiet and peace, the peace they talked about in church, a peace that surpassed her understanding. She would have run to the church but she knew all too well she would not find any peace there. If only she could have talked to God alone at the church, she would have found peace. But no, she would have to answer too many questions because some people are so religious minded they're no earthly good. She needed silence. She needed to block out every damaging and damning word and every angry blow of the world she was running from. She needed to hear her Jesus answer her prayer.

She thought of running to the park where she could sit on the green grass under the trees, look to the skies, and become part of God's creation. This is where she always found peace and God, but he would have found her there, just as he had the time before, and the time before that, crying, wounded, battered, and alone. But this time she would not be talked back, lured back, dragged back into a world that had no hope, no joy, no love, and no peace. This time she would break free. This time she would not fall on her knees in surrender and plead for help to anyone but Jesus.

She had saved and hidden every penny she could out of her meager salary. Her husband kept a tight rein on how much she made and how she spent it. He knew she realized money was her gateway to freedom, but he had to work, so he allowed her to work, as well. He did not have to like it, however. She was his slave and he was her jealous overseer.

She made up excuses to try to hide her money from him. She would tell him she lost it, or someone stole it, or she'd say she had to contribute some to mandatory birthday pots at the office. She told every lie she could think of to finally buy her freedom. She learned how to do her own hair and nails and became an expert at finding bargains. She learned to save coupons for all the household needs and groceries, anything to keep as much money for herself as she could.

Once when he was collecting her part of the bill, she told him, "I gave five dollars to a homeless mother and child." But that only earned her a berating and a slap across the face.
"How you gonna give somebody money?" he chided. "You'd be homeless if it wasn't for me. I own this house and everything in it, including you."

She decided to go the bus terminal. She would be safe there, and she wouldn't be alone. There would be people coming and going anywhere and everywhere. They had freedom. Cloaking herself in a headscarf and sunglasses did very little to hide her shame, or was it really his?

She ducked and dodged through side streets and corners, knowing he would be looking for her. She had been so careful in hiding her escape money, her exchange for freedom. But when she arrived home from work that day, it was gone from the sewn hem of the old coat in the back of the closet. She said nothing. He watched her all that evening through dinner, quiet, fuming with a rage he could not hide behind his smugness. She wondered whether he could smell her freedom like she could.

She was ready to risk life and limb to be free, though she told no one but Jesus in whispered prayers. "Pray to Jesus," she remembered her mother teaching her, because Jesus hears our prayers and answers them. Her mother was whispering Jesus' name the night she died. She remembered praying "Now lay me down to sleep; I pray the Lord my soul to keep,"[38] crying "Mommy, wake up and pray with me," while her small arms bore the weight of her mother's bludgeoned and bloody body. With her tear-stained face she watched as the police took her drunken handcuffed father away. That was the last time she saw him--fourteen years ago. She was only four years old when her father killed her mother. Afterward, she was left alone, with only the legacy of feeling dead like her mother, and handcuffed to the state foster care system because of her father's violent and selfish act. All she had was a child's memory of a bedtime prayer and the promise that Jesus answers prayers.

She found a bench in the bus terminal where she could see the entrance and an easy access to escape. She knew he would be looking for her. She tried to get away before but he always found her. She thought of the police but they could not help. After all, they did not help her mother. Her only way to freedom was to run far away this time to a place where he could not find her. Peeping through the small slits she formed with her eyes when she closed them halfway, too afraid to close them completely, she whispered to Jesus, "Please forgive me for lying." She saw no other way to save her freedom money. "Jesus, I need you," she pleaded. "I can't do this alone." How would she exist? She never remembered living, only existing, though sometimes she experienced glimpses of what living actually felt like. "Jesus, if I die before I wake, my soul I give to you to take; I'm tired." She had no one. After all, she had never been loved by anyone other than her mother and Jesus. "Jesus, take me home with you. Can I see my mother?"

She heard a rustling sound and looked up to see an old lady, dressed poorly, sit down on the bench beside her. She knew it was rude to stare, but the old lady had scars scattered all over her forehead, neck, arms, hands, and even her feet, which demanded her attention. Frightened, she clung to the edge of the bench; finally she was able to look away. She sat on that bench for hours, drifting in and out of sleep. Each time she awoke she was disappointed she was not in heaven, but each time she saw the old lady at the other end of the bench, rocking back and forth, speaking soft, inaudible words to her.

---

[38] A classic children's prayer from the 18th century, printed in The New England Primer.

Finally the old lady said "I been watching you while you slept and while you waked and while you prayed. I come to this bus station every day, watching and observing people as they go about their lives. I can look into their faces and see and hear their stories, some good and some bad. Everybody got a story, some with happy outcomes and some with tragic ends. I've heard folks speaking every name you could imagine, seeking help. With all this technology you can call anybody from anywhere for anything. Oh but today, baby, you brought this old woman joy 'cause out of your mouth I heard you call the name 'Jesus'. Not like those fools who call 'Jesus' in a thoughtless exclamation out of frustration 'cause they running late or because they children won't sit still; no, there was no vainness in your calling upon the name of Jesus. You meant it, you felt it, and you sat in expectancy for Jesus to come. Like I said, I been watching you hiding behind them shades, all covered up trying to hide your scars. You running, ain't you? Tired of fighting? I know your story because I lived it and I got a scar for every chapter. I was a fighting Viking, too, and I got the scars to prove it."

The old lady began pointing to each scar, as she recounted chapter after chapter of each story in her life, ranging from bar fights, brutish men, and evil women, to a house fire that almost took her life. Then she pointed to her knee and said, "See, this scar here I got it saving my child. By the time he was born I had straighten my life up. I thought I was through getting scars. One day my child was riding his tricycle and out of nowhere this drunken fool in a car come barreling through our yard. With no thought, I was ready to give up my own life for his, and these are the scars to prove it. Our scars bear witness to our stories; they tell where we've been. Jesus' scars, they tell where we are going. Jesus' scars are living proof that he died and lives again, so that we might live more abundantly. It's in His Word. Look at me; I bear my scars proudly. My scars are medals of victory through my Jesus. You ain't got to fight no more; let Jesus do your fighting. It ain't no shame in running, baby; it's a shame if you don't know to run to Jesus. Now I can see you need help, and I am here to help you. My name is Ettie.[39] Here, see my card."

She took the card, too exhausted to say her name. "It don't matter who looking for you as long as you look to Jesus," Ettie continued. "We'll talk about it, get it all straight tomorrow; you got a new future to plan." Having no money and nowhere to go, the girl got up and followed Ettie. She looked at the card she held in her hand, and it read "Strong Tower Mission--Bear Your Scars; They are Medals of Testimony--Jesus Hears, Jesus Loves, and Jesus Saves."[40]

Two women, one old and one young, both fighting Vikings bearing scars, as their Lord and Savior did, one who had already learned and one who was learning the saving grace of Philippians 4:6-7: "Be anxious for nothing, but in everything by prayer and supplication, with thanksgiving, let your requests be made known to God; and the peace of God, which surpasses all understanding, will guard your hearts and minds through Christ Jesus."

---

[39]Ettie is a Persian variant of Esther that means "noble," "myrtle leaf," or "home ruler."
[40]Psalm 61:3, "For thou hast been a shelter for me, and a strong tower from the enemy."

"I Love Me Some Him, Hymn, and HIM: A Trilogy"

I

They say music calms the wild beast. Many believe classical music stimulates the mind, and many swear "the blues" or the "blue devils," conjures up emotions best left alone. But all music, whether instrumental or worded; whether jazz or rhythm and blues; or whether classical, country, rock, or rap, interprets the writer's or the poet's owned or observed experience.

But there is something about a hymn, about Gospel music, that takes on the likeness and characteristics of God. The writer's experience, the concept of a creation being formed by the spiritual intimacy of thoughts, memories, feelings, and visions, produces a creative power that grows within the writer and gives birth to a testimony in psalm. It speaks of life and tells of the saving mercy and grace of God. And because the lyrics or melodies are birthed from memoirs of the holy Word, they bring the Holy Spirit into our presence.

The first chapter of Genesis gives an account of how God created the earth and all therein. Chapter two talks about the creation of the first man, Adam, and the first woman, Eve, who was created for him. Chapter three details Adam and Eve's disobedience to God's Word and their resultant fall. But before all this occurred, God said "Let there be light." I find it awe-inspiring that God gives us enlightenment and examples of how to receive His power, and that when we use His Word, our words can bring light to any dark situation.

II
Elle "She"

This is a story of a woman, named Elle, which means "she," and refers to something traditionally known or previously mentioned in the feminine gender, such as a "nation." Elle comes from the Hebrew name "Elizabeth" (*Elisheva)* and also means, "sun ray," "shining light," "God's promise," and "God is my oath." The Hebrew form appears in the Old Testament where Elisheba is the wife of Aaron, while the Greek form appears in the New Testament where Elizabeth is the mother of John the Baptist.

Every woman will love one man unconditionally, someone she encounters for the first time and cries in her heart, "That's him!" because she knows she was created just for him, like Eve was created for Adam. How they choose to live their lives, in obedience or disobedience to God's Word, determines whether they will live in God's promise and establishes the power of their dominion. In obedience their Garden of Eden is created. In disobedience they become foreigners to each other and to God. In exile, they are banished from their perfect garden.

As she readied herself for morning service, Elle turned the radio to the Gospel station. She remembered how this home was once full of music, laughter, love, and prayers, as she and her husband prepared for a day of worshipping the Lord together. From the rafter to the floorboards, their home sang "Remember the Sabbath day and keep it holy"[41] every day. She was led by a Joshua 24:15 man ("And if it seems evil to you to serve the LORD, choose for yourselves..."). But somewhere between love and good-bye they lost holy and happy, and their home became only a house.

She waited a long time to marry. She was never man crazy, just crazy about her man. She did not just want a man to live with; she wanted a man she could not live without. As Elle picked up her Bible, she grabbed her purse and locked the door.

She thought of her mother's words: "I gave you this name because I wanted you to have it better than me and the others. I wanted you to be kindred with your namesake. Marry you a good Godly man, maybe even a preacher, and birth out some children that would stand up and live for Jesus."

As she backed out of the garage and drove away from the house that was once a divine blessing, Elle thought about how Eve must have felt, knowing she was created for a certain man for God's purpose to be fulfilled and yet falling short. She must have felt such anguish to know that by her trespassing, she had entered into a knowledge as forbidden as the fruit she caused her and her husband to eat. She had let evil slither in on its belly to plant seeds of deceit, lies, deception, and conflict in her home. Elle thought of Proverbs 14:1: "Every wise woman buildeth her house: but the foolish plucketh it down with her hands." She thought, "Poor Eve; poor me."

Adam and Eve must have been filled with so much guilt and shame, as they walked out of their Eden. They must have avoided each other's fault-finding eyes. After all, she was out of order and led; he, the man, was out of order, too, because he followed even though he was the first. She wondered whether this was the first time a woman received relief from her song. She imagined Eve starting to groan and moan with the agony of what she had done, so ashamed and spiritually wounded that all she could do was moan, "um... hum...O," or was Adam the first to cry out a hymn in repentance? Or did they grip their disgrace together, as they walked hand and hand out of the garden? Did they hear the birds and the bees weep a melody as they departed, or hear the wind's soft breeze through the trees turn against them into a shrilling scream of grief?

Or was the first song birthed out with the searing pain of contractions in childbirth, with grunts and moans as her body inhaled death to breathe out new life, knowing with a mother's instinct the seed would eventually bring them to another bitter end? Was this the first time a woman embraced God through a hymn? Genesis 3:15 says, "And I will put enmity between you and the woman, and between your seed and her Seed; He shall bruise your head, and you shall bruise His heel."

---

[41]The 4th commandment, "Remember [zachor] the Sabbath day and keep it holy" (Deuteronomy reads shamor, meaning to "observe"")

Her Him

Somewhere between love and good-bye, Elle found she and her man had been banished from their Eden, and no matter how many times they tried to return, a flaming sword[42] blocked their entrance. Throughout her life, Elle had known a few men who melted her heart and captured her mind. Even fewer inspired her and ignited her soul. But he, this exceptional man, if only to her, was "her him." He managed to do all these things at once, not systematically, but symphonically, harmonious in every way imaginable. She adored him, told him so, and meant with every fiber of her soul that if she had been born a man she would have wanted to be just like him, for he was mirrored in God's image, the spirit of God in man. She saw so much of Jesus' sweetness in him. If only to her, "her him" was magnificent. Doesn't every woman see her man that way if she truly loves him?

Later she realized perhaps her love was so exceptional because she fell in love with "her him" at the same time she fell in love with Jesus. This was also about the same time she became wise enough to know the difference between romancing Jesus and loving Him unconditionally. She laughed to herself thinking how foolish and how unfair it was to place her man on a pedestal so high he would never be able to stay on top, or climb back up when he fell off of it. But as she pulled into the church parking lot, she still had so many questions, and still not enough answers.

III
At the Sunday Service

Church had already started when Elle arrived, so she walked to the back pews and sat quietly. As she looked around the sanctuary, she saw herself, a nation of "she's" between love and good-bye, and wondered if she had become one of them.

When did she begin to equate him (her man) with Hymn (the song), and Him (the Almighty God)? Was that when she began to see "her him" in a brand new light? Somewhere in the darkness of her ignorance, she realized "her him" was merely a man trying to understand, embrace, and come forth in God's plan just like her and so many others. And somewhere in the darkness, she saw herself in a revealing light, the Him in her. She pondered this as she began to let Hymn become the courier of Him, and woo her with words of love and incontestable proof that her other "him" could not equal Him, and she could not deny her love for the Him who saved her. She would always be indebted and thankful to Hymn for pointing the way to Him's words of instruction that taught her how to really breathe, how to really live, and how to really give life and love.

[42]Genesis 3:24: "So...and a flaming sword which turned every way"

She had now joined the ranks of other women followers of Him. She went to sleep and woke up with Him on her mind, Him in her heart, and the words of Hymn ringing in her ears, raging in her belly until she thought she would burst. No matter how she tried to quiet her spirit, praises of Hymn flowed out of her mouth.

At first "the other him" (her man) was so pleased that she had become a good, submissive, church girl. But soon, both began forgetting to live and love by the rest of the scriptures of Ephesians 5:20-33: "Giving thanks always for all things unto God…Nevertheless let every one of you in particular so love his wife even as himself; and the wife see that she reverence her husband." This is when that old serpent began to plant his seed of separation in him and in her. As time passed, she began to see a jealousy grow and a competition fester between "her him" and "her Him." It was not enough for her man to know she loved him because of her God, and no matter how many times she declared her love to him, they grew more and more distant from one another. She told him that if she had lived in Biblical times, she would have been one of Jesus' women followers, fetched His water, washed His feet with her hair, and laid at the cross and wept for Him.

Because of this revelation she embodied 1 Corinthians 13:4-7 (KJV): "Love is patient; love is kind; love is not envious…." She rejoiced in the truth and would bear all things, believe all things, hope all things, and endure all things. He was her husband and her vows were sacred. Even when others tried to persecute him, judge him, or crucify him, she would never deny him, leave him, nor forsake him. But after that conversation, "her him" only saw her words as second-hand love instead of words and love imaged and seeded by Him.

Somewhere between love and good-bye, both of them had missed something. If only they had stood on God's Word. If only they had smashed that old serpent's seed before it took hold. All she ever wanted was for them to be the new and improved, obedient image of Adam and Eve. Romans 8:6 says, "For to be carnally minded is death, but to be spiritual minded is life and peace." So many questions…still not enough answers.

So now, Elle sits quietly near the last pews, sporting one of her many strained smiles, among the parading rows of beautiful pearly white teeth hiding the ugly truth, and barricading a scream for help. When had she become part of the iconic constant reminder of the causes and effects of carnal love, instead of submitting to the power of spiritual love? Now, she had become a woman waiting for Hymn to usher in Him and breathe life into her suffocating spirit.

As she sat in the pews, the song she heard sounded like the broken-hearted woman's Hymn. Or perhaps it was a woman's "Lord, I can't do this by myself" poem of true, long-lasting love. You see, the sweet words of "I Come to the Garden Alone" fill the vacancy inside a lonely heart. A few bars of "Peace Be Still "quiets the tormented mind. Sitting, praying, and waiting for the words, "Pass Me Not Oh Gentle Savior" lifts the spirit out of depression with a new-found hope, while believers of the Word wait and trust their praises would cause God to inhabit them.[43]

She sat there, and in her mind, transported back to those times as a little girl when a request in the form of a small white piece of paper, neatly folded and perfectly squared, would be ushered somewhere from the pews, as an atmosphere of espionage infiltrated the service. Row after row, the congregation became parishioners of surveillance, intelligence, and counter-intelligence as the note was passed. Sometimes this would occur in the midst of a fiery sermon and Hallelujahs. Sometimes it would arise from whispered "Amens" and sighs mingled with tears.

In the midst of this well–trained, strategically laid-out convoy, an emissary dressed in an all white uniform took delivery of the guarded memo, the head usher military erect, right arm behind her back, left arm respectfully raised, and head bowed. She held a note of hope and need in reverence, with her finger pointed upward, as a transformation occurred. The dwelling place was seized by a steeled hush and the stillness escorted in supernatural armor. Helmets and breastplates replaced peacock bonnets and garments. No longer were there turned heads, wandering eyes, impatient clearing of throats, and the crossing and uncrossing of legs. No longer was there under-breath sanctimonious speculations or the squirming and pulling of too-tight clothes and even tighter shoes. Now, yes now, sat and stood soldiers on every side, girded in truth.

As the congregation watched and listened attentively, the sanctuary assumed a position of confident expectancy, being strong in the Lord, like Ephesians 6:10-17 (KJV) says: "finally, my brethren, be strong in the Lord and in the power of His might. Put on the whole armor of God that you may be able to stand against the wiles of the devil…."

As the note completed the final leg of its destination, from head usher to the pastor to the choir stand, finally, the music began. Ms. Lou raised her bowed head, stood her soldier-worn body, and began to sing "For every mountain you brought me over, for every trial you seen me through" and that hymn ushered down the Holy Spirit into every downtrodden soul. Words of "I sing hallelujah; thank you, Jesus; for this I give you praise" were laid at His feet, and the hand of God began to caress and smooth out the deepest wrinkles of the most crumpled heart. Elle was so relieved, she could finally breathe. Past memories confirmed her faith. Elle would let Hymn and Him minister to her heart, just like the other "she's" had before her. Another love story gone wrong; another woman learned to let man be man, and let God be God.

All questions can be answered by the holy Word. Psalm 119:60 says that it is absolutely sufficient in itself. "And the peace of God, which passeth all understanding, shall keep your hearts and minds through Christ Jesus," says Philippians 4:7. There is a Mexican Proverb I have always loved: "The house does not rest upon the ground, but upon a woman." But I now believe a home rests upon a praying obedient woman and a praying obedient man.

[43]Psalm 22:3 "But thou art holy, O thou that inhabits the praises of Israel."

[44]"For Every Mountain," original by Kurt Carr.

[45]Ibid.

"Don't judge each day by the harvest you reap but by the seeds that you plant."

--Robert Louis Stevenson

"Interview with a Preacher Man and a Preacher Woman"

Dedicated to all the Family Ministries of the Gospel
(Poem/skit with three speakers: 1.The reporter, 2. The husband, and 3. The wife. The reporter's speech is in bold, the husband's is in plain text, and the wife's is in italic.)

I

As I sat before them I could feel yet another's presence.
Familiar yet comfortingly strange
And there was a fragrance So-o-o sweet which is only attained in Jesus' name
What could I ask this profound couple, who had shared a lifetime of saving souls?
Who bowed humbly before the Lord, forsaking all others to have and to hold
Yoked by a calling to deliver the Word to set men free
Providing mankind with anointed liberties

II

Preacher Man! Preacher Woman!
This was a tedious walk you chose, how did God
lead you to this awesome place?
It is utterly prudent that this reporter states,

The room was instantly filled with angelic voices speaking of overwhelming love
The atmosphere then changed to something more powerful sent down from above
I rather be a door keeper in the house of the Lord than to have lived another life
And it has been an honor to be in God's service
To have such a godly husband, to have such a godly wife

III

Preacher Man! Preacher Woman!
How does it come that all your children are saved? And yet again their unity of matrimony
was anchored in unison of praise.

As for me and my house
We will serve the Lord at all times Rise early in the morning; anoint your house from
dissension and contempt
He who fell to the outermost is consumed with hatred and jealousy
Safeguard your home and hearts from deception
For he comes to steal, kill, and destroy you and me

IV

I am an example of loving-kindness, never forgetting why Jesus wept
Meekness is my virtue; The Lord Jesus is my crown; This is where salvation is abundantly found
Teach your daughters to bind their tongues of tale-bearing, for it is a most uncomely sin
To wait on the Lord Jesus to present them with a true and righteous man

V
In my sons I planted a seed

The strength and gentleness, which a woman needs
To set the tone of a sanctified home
In which God and the family is pleased

That it is not the laying,
But the praying on the knees
That institutes the Father's heavenly deeds

For a mate is to be chosen wisely,
As not to suffer harm
"This" is what gives comfort in a wintery storm
VI
Preacher Man! Preacher Woman!
What would you tell a travailing world?

Women of struggle and Men in trouble
Lean not to your own understandings and do not be dismayed
Remember the Ten Commandments
Practice them every single day
The Almighty sits high and looks low
Keep your eyes on the prize;
Sing through your storm
This is what will protect you from harm

VII
There is no greater comfort than found in Jesus' arms
And through all things you are a conqueror free from alarm

VIII
The God we serve leaves nothing lacking, missing, or broken.
Remember--He sits high and looks low
And without praise and supplication a sinner man's soul will never righteously flow

Cast your sins and iniquities upon the Red Sea
Rely not to your own understanding, for God said
"Lean solely on Me"

Be not a man of whims and fancies

In the end these worldly gifts are thimble held
And yes, my children, there surely is a Heaven
And yes, my children, there surely is a Hell

Written and first recited for Apostle Dennis Cook and President Marilyn Cook of Mt. Zion Transformation Center in Texarkana, Texas/Arkansas, honoring their anniversary in 2008.

"It's that He Prayed With Me"

I

It was not the way his lips brushed my ear as he kissed it
And spoke words of secrets that only we and God shared

II

It was not the strength of his fingers which seem to fit the small of my back
As we shared an embrace of good-bye
Or the lingering fragrance of his manly scent that stayed with me all through the day
It was just that he always prayed with me
III
Of all the memories of love and its possibilities, capabilities, ecstasies, and agonies
Of all these things he will forever to me be the essence of the spirit of God in man to me
I tell you, it is simply because he knelt down on his knees, bowed his head,
And laid the ego of man at the foot of the cross and at our Master's feet;
And surrendered himself to God
And he prayed with me.

IV

I am of the Shulamite Woman[46] and he is of the Shepherd Lover
With each prayer we are becoming the honey and the honeycomb
Simply because…
My love prayed with me.
***

Who would you choose to be, Solomon or the shepherd lover? Women, would you choose to be one of Solomon's many wives or the Shulamite woman? I would choose to be the latter for both. There is blesseth peace, joy, and Godly prosperity in a union rooted in fidelity and honor.

---

[46]Song of Solomon, Chapter 1. Eros is the physical, sensual love between a husband and wife.

"God always gives His best to those who leave the choice with Him."
---Jim Elliot
***

"I, too…have always known that my destiny was, above all, a literary destiny--that bad things and some good things would happen to me, but that, in the long run, all of it would be converted into words. Particularly the bad things, since happiness does not need to be transformed: happiness is its own end."
--Jorge Luis Borges

CHAPTER III

DON'T LIMIT YOUR LIFE TO WHISPERS

The Word says, "Our gifts make room for us." God gives us gifts in all forms and those gifts become our ministries when we use them to spread the Good News.

Cheerleading Journalism

Below is an excerpt of an article that appeared in the Texarkana Community Journal (TCJ), a community newspaper founded and managed by Pastor Paul Keener of Texarkana, Texas.[47] He and his staff, some of whom volunteer, are like so many newspaper ministries throughout our country that work diligently every day to spread the Good News of the Gospel, as well as inform and enlighten their communities of national, civic, and church events. They operate solely by support and donations from their communities and benefactors.

This article, "Am I My Sister's Keeper? Yes I Am," focuses on the abuse of women and children, particularly one courageous woman, Dr. Sandy Murphy, a noted author and advocate for abuse prevention and recovery, who allowed me to tell her story. It should be well noted that many men suffer from abuse every day. If you or someone you know is experiencing domestic abuse, I implore you to seek counseling. There are local ministries, organizations, and agencies that can help you, and as civic-minded members of society, we should consider gifts of financial support to such ministries. I, too, am a survivor, so together let's let the healing begin!

"Am I My Sister's Keeper? Yes I Am!"

by Sandra Dukes

There is an epidemic that has seized our nation much too long. Its symptoms are exhibited in the form of raised ferocious fists, brutal kicks, and cruel threatening words. The plague of domestic violence is cloaked within vindictive and malicious emotional

---

[47]Paul Keener is the Senior Pastor of Hickory Hill Baptist Church in Nash, Texas, and a civic leader in his community.

and physical mistreatment, resulting in the death of not only the body but also the spirit and the soul!

These acts of violent behavior are strangling our people of their integrity and divine purpose. We are producing generation upon generation of a populace birthed from wounded wombs. One might ask themselves, "What can I do? Why would anyone subject themselves to such treatment?" The answer to this question should be approached like any other. First we must recognize and admit there is a problem, explore the cause with research and education to seek a solution, and then and only then can the healing begin. Again you may ask yourself if this infliction does not touch your life, "Why should I bear the duty, assume the responsibility?"

Throughout history when we as a people have ignored the injustices of others, it has tragically affected us as a whole. These atrocities have spanned time from the Native Americans' "trail of tears," to robbing Africa of its sons and daughters and imprisoning them into slavery, to Japanese American internment, to [the] hate crimes of today. These aggressions against mankind have scarred our nation. I contend that yes, we are our brothers' and our sisters' keepers. I also contend that the atrocities aforementioned are no more or no less than the scourge of abuse that plagues and threatens to destroy our children and our women. If we approach this dilemma from a spiritual perspective, all that is required is to read and meditate on these words in the Bible:

> And the Lord said unto Cain, Where is Abel thy brother? And he said, I know not: Am I my brother's keeper? And he [God] said, what hast thou done? The voice of thy brother's blood crieth unto me from the ground (Genesis 4:9-10 (KJV)).

The blood of our brother is now our sister's and it is still crying out to be heard! We must band together and be a voice of rescue and active reform. We should have a sense of duty not only because it is beneficial to our well-being; we should reach out because it is decent, moral, and loving. We must become the remedy that will cure this disease that has infested our families, communities, and nation.

On September 6, 1974, at age 18, Dr. Sandy Murphy, mother of two, was shot by her husband between the eyes at close range with a twelve-gauge shotgun. Even though the entire right side of her face was almost blown completely away, she miraculously survived.

Dr. Murphy is her sister's keeper. She is one of the vessels from which God's anointing flows to administer an antidote to the poison of domestic violence that infects and affects us all. Dr. Murphy, minister and noted author in Houston, Texas, a survivor, knows too well the effects of this crime against body and soul. She is a healer of the heart and spirit who offers her services through Sandy Murphy Ministries at the School Ministry & Mentoring Academy, and her blog talk radio show "Dr. Keeping It Real." Dr. Murphy also hosts her television show "Real Sessions with Sandy" on the Houston Access Cable Media Source.

"Do they still call it infatuation? That magic ax that chops away the world in one blow, leaving only the couple standing there trembling? Whatever they call it, it leaps over anything, takes the biggest chair, the largest slice, rules the ground wherever it walks, from a mansion to a swamp, and its selfishness is its beauty...People with no imagination feed it with sex--the clown of love. They don't know the real kinds, the better kinds, where losses are cut and everybody benefits. It takes a certain intelligence to love like that--softly, without props."

--Toni Morrison, Paradise

***

"Be a Ruth not Ruth-less with your love."

--Sandra Dukes

***

"For as he thinks in his heart, so is he. "Eat and drink!" he says to you, But his heart is not with you."

--Proverbs 23:7 (NKJV)

"Chocolate Thunder"
A Play in Poetic Form and Song

For many years, chocolate was believed to be an aphrodisiac because it contains phenylephylamine, the same hormone the brain triggers when we fall in love. Thunder is the sound caused by lightning. A thunderstorm is a storm that contains lightning and thunder, which is caused by unstable atmospheric conditions. A man of this character is continually distracted. He will neither let earth nor heaven go, and yet he can only have one. This man's soul is divided in two: one soul for earth and one for heaven because he wishes to secure both worlds. But James 1:8 (KJV) says, "A double-minded man is unstable in all his ways." Our lives and the lives of others should never be taken lightly. We are more than characters, rhymes, and lyrics. We are born with divine purposes set by God.

Stanza 1/Act 1

Casanova, Romeo, Heartbreaker, Gigolo--Oh You Sliver-Tongued Devil You!

The stage is set with broken hearts
Broken promises, your deceiving Art
Sometimes Bitter, Sometimes Sweet
Thespis[48] candied miseries

A script of lies, impending part
Delivered by an empty heart
The billboard flashes
"Romance Tragedy--
Operatic Slaying of Destinies"

I see lightning! I hear thunder
It makes me wonder
Where you gonna lay your head tonight?

---

[48]Greek word THESPIAN/Hypokrites: Named for Thespis, who played an important part in the history of Greek drama, believed by some to be the first person to speak lines onstage instead of singing them.

Stanza 2/Act2

The scene is set high on a bridge
He is mine; I am his
Vowing to take the plunge
Hopelessly in love we run
We leap--I scream
Only God hears
Chocolate Thunder has disappeared!

He flipped the script, giving no notice
Hypocrite, his love was bogus
He took me to soaring heights
Leaving me--crashing--midflight

It makes me wonder…
How many bodies have taken this fall?
Choosing love or nothing at all

I'm not looking for a bungee-jump lover I said "I'm not looking for a bungee-jump lover."

Bridge/Climax

Disbursing hurt; dispensing pain
Today's fame; tomorrow's shame
For what is a lover-man between the sheets, but a single woman for the devil to defeat?
Hey Chocolate Thunder
You make me wonder
Where you gonna lay--where you gonna lay--
Where you laying your head tonight?
I'm not looking for a bungee-jump lover
I said "I 'm not looking for a bungee-jump lover"
Hey Chocolate Thunder; where you laying your head tonight?
Casanova, Romeo, Heartbreaker, Gigolo--Oh You Sliver-Tongued Devil You!

Stanza 3 /Finale

The Curtain is closed
The Lights are down
The critics are gossiping all over town
"Are you just a misunderstood man;
Or a man with a thespian plan;
Hell-bent in bringing chocolate clouds into a sister's day?"

I pray someday blind eyes see
The more God created you to Be

Honor, Truth, Integrity
"God bless your little heart"[49]
Where are you laying your head tonight?

Stanza 4/Poetic
Narrator's Review / Prophetic Scribe's Warning

Single Women--Single Men
Sex without matrimony is a sin
Beware of Lust masquerading as Love
Sexual Genocide and all of its culprits

Married Women--Married Men
Stop lying about your marital status
Involving others in your adulterous havoc
With each soul-tie that you take
You compromise someone else's fate
Take heed of your melodrama part
A trickster's killing of innocent hearts

The Earth is quaking for a moral awakening
"Where are you laying your head tonight?"
I see lightning! I hear thunder!
The heavens rumble
"Where are you laying your head tonight?"

---

[49] "Bless your little heart" is a term used by the people of the southern United States, particularly near the Gulf of Mexico, to express that someone is a fool or acting foolishly, without using harsh words.

"Thy tongue deviseth mischiefs; like a sharp razor, working deceitfully. Thou lovest evil more than good; and lying rather than to speak righteousness. Selah. Thou lovest all devouring words, O thou deceitful tongue."

--Psalm 52:2-4 (KJV)

***

"A man or woman not satisfied with one mate will not be satisfied with many for the discontentment is within themselves."

--Sandra Dukes

***

"Life itself is a quotation."

--Jorge Luis Borges

"Crooked Living"

There was a crooked man
Who walked a crooked mile
He had a crooked heart
He lived a crooked style
He spoke crooked words
With a crooked tongue
So everything he dreamed was crooked before it begun.
There was a crooked man who had a crooked wife
So everywhere they lived they lived a crooked life

Poem adapted from the limerick, "There was a Crooked Man," the origins of which originated from the English Stuart history of King Charles I. Limericks and nursery rhymes often reflected events in history. Many words and lyrics from these poems and songs were used as metaphoric satire since direct dissent was not allowed. As a writer and an adult in North America, I find it interesting how the childhood memory of a British nursery rhyme can be effective in observing life situations.

"One of the most powerful legacies we can receive from family comes in the form of storytelling. These stories are told as morality and cautionary lessons to live one's life to its full potential."

--Jorge Luis Borges

CHAPTER IV

GENERATIONAL BLESSINGS

"PORTRAIT OF A BLACK SPIRIT"

Black Awareness Day, Juneteenth, was initially a one-day celebration in my hometown of Corpus Christi, Texas, but it grew in proportion and fame to a week of events, entertainment, and celebration of our African–American heritage. People of all racial and ethnic cultures in the community and state were encouraged to become involved in the recognition of African–American heritage. This celebration presented creative abilities, skills, and talents where scholarships were funded from the proceeds.

Dorothy Benson,[50] the founder of the Juneteenth celebration in Corpus Christi and a born futurist, had the vision of celebrating the uniqueness of the African–Americans' contributions to fashion. At that time I was a professional model and airline flight attendant. Dorothy (Dottie) presented her project to me and I embraced it. Each year for several years I returned home to choreograph and participate in the Black Awareness Day fashion segment. Laura Crawford Jones (whose last name is now Henderson) proved to be more than my assistant and one of the production's lead models. She always had the necessary preparations completed, and we began auditioning, training, and rehearsing the local talent for the upcoming showcase. By the grace of God, with each year that passed, the fashion segment increased. What started as a performance in one of the city's parks was soon featured at our city's beautiful Convention Center. The last Black Awareness Day, during which we as the original team performed together, was a fashion extravaganza. "Portrait of a Black Spirit" was an elegant evening featuring a fashion production (including designer), jazz music, dancing, a down-home food taste, and an art gallery where items could be purchased. What I find most gratifying is that through the efforts of the Black Awareness Committee and all of its participants and sponsors, others later carried the torch and inspired others throughout their families, professions, and civic lives.

June nineteenth is the date of the emancipation of black slaves in the state of Texas. The rebirth of Juneteenth was due in part to our celebrations in Corpus Christi. Junteenth is now recognized as an official state holiday and is being celebrated in states by Texans wherever they are now living.

---

[50] Retired Professor Dorothy Benson–Brown is one of my dearest friends, first mentor and creative muse. Her story is quite unique in itself, from maid to mentor to college professor. Dottie has devoted her life to inspiring her children, family, her students, and community to reach unreachable stars.

Following is the poem, "Inspire Me to Be," which I wrote and dedicated to Dorothy during the performance of "Portrait of a Black Spirit." It embodies my sentiments of   Dorothy's vision . The poem was dedicated and performed at the Juneteenth Ceremony at the Corpus Christi Convention Center in 1983. Since then, this poem has evolved into yet another poem that has crossed racial, gender, and chronological lines and expresses the gratitude and appreciation for those who inspire others to embrace their gifts from God and each other[51] because the roll call goes on and on and on, giving God all the glory!

"Inspire Me to Be"

Dedicated to the founder of Black Awareness Day
Dorothy Benson
I
I have inherited a fortune--that cannot be compared
For it rose from ancient earth and comets throughout the hemisphere
It is a legend--The Black Woman's Treasure--This Golden Chest
Overflowing with the most precious jewels--robbed from Africa's breast
Brutalized--Taunted--And Possessed
Taught to worship material things
Forced to forget our men once were Kings
With nothing but the Lord-God on our side
We have not faltered our spirits vividly alive
Descendants of Nefertiti Sheba Cleopatra Aunt Jemima, and Annie Jean[52]
Mothers of struggle singing "Pass Me Not Oh Gentle Savior Hear My Humble Cry"
He Heard
Evolving silent screams into Fulfilled Dreams

II
Yes this legend is a bountiful treasure! Sensitive and Rare
For I am of a soulful blackness; a classic beauty only my sisters share
And while sitting by a Carolina fire this wisdom came to me
Women of your ingredients inspire me to write poetry
For we are who we are a reflection of our pride
A Spiritual banner for our guide
Waving defiantly in the air soaring beyond the skies
Proclaiming the unsung tale of how we The Mother-Seed came from bondage to rise!

III
Inspire me Inspire Me to Be
Roll Call--Harriet Phyllis Sojourner Maya Ella Coretta Angela Naomi The Annie Lees[53]

---

[51]"A Tribute to Cheerleaders for a Better World: Inspiration Revisited in Cryptic Prose"
[52]Mother of Sandra Dukes.
[53]Great grandmother of Sandra Dukes.

the Nikki G's And Tina T's Corpus Christi's own LeLe, Eartha Shirley Yvonne Eunice Dorothy
Ruby Dee Josephine Billie Della Pearl Rosa The Boss Ms. Ross Marva Leontyne The Jane
Pittmans Aretha Sarah Ethel Marian Mahalia And the roll call goes on
And you Dottie
Inspire Me Inspire Me to Be
And the Roll Call goes on and on and on and on...

The next two poems, "Le Bonbons'" and "Hambone, Hambone," were narrated and choreographed in "Portrait of a Black Spirit" to celebrate the uniqueness and beauty of the color spectrum and heritage of African Americans.

"Le Bonbons"

Toffee candy what a treat
Brown Sugar Lassie, Carmel heat
Honey Gold baby sweet enough to eat
Peach–Skinned Girlie
Coffee
Cream
Chocolate Darling out of a dream

The next rhyme publicly acknowledges the gratitude and the honor that should be given to black men (and women) who, in the early part of the twentieth century, had to leave their homes to find jobs in order to make better lives for their families. These men occupied industrial positions up North, joined the military, or held jobs on military installations, such as the one in Corpus Christi. Facing racial and economical prejudices and dangers, they trudged on

.

"Hambone"[34]
Hambone, Hambone!
What you be?
For you to know and for them to see!
Hambone, Hambone
Where you heading?
To find a place where love is spreading!
Hambone, Hambone
Where you been?
Around the world and back again!
Hambone, Hambone
Your women are proud and they understand
Your troubles, your struggles for being a black man!

---

[34] Inspired by the song HAMBONE by Red Saunders, Leon Washington, and Bill Haley

"All my family, my blood, is mixed up now. They don't even all know each other. I just hope they don't never hate or fight each other, not knowin' who they are. 'Cause all these people livin' are brothers and sisters and cousins. All these beautiful different colors…We!…We are the human Family. God says so! Family!"

--*J. California Cooper, Family*

"It's Been So Hard Being Me" is written in Visual or Shape Verse. This style of writing has been around almost as long as writing itself. It is a poet's deliberate attempt to communicate to the reader through the image of the placement of the words as well as the meaning of the words. I pray my attempt has been successful and the reader will be able to identify with the plight of the speaker in this poem.

"It's Been So Hard Being Me"

**It's been so hard being me. I tell you, it's been
so hard being me**

You see before I was colored
I was a **nigger** a **Negra**, a **black**. This depending on if I was being addressed by an illiterate or refined **bigot**.

Then **God** must have shamed them in to renaming me into a **Nee-gro**
        Now-- I was alright with that Then I thought –maybe it wasn't
shame or God But the *Spaniards* because the word Negro Means **Black** in *Spanish* I've
been *defined* and *dissected* into so many parts of *explanations* of my **treatment**
In so many *variations* of *degrees* and *colors* I almost forgot *me, myself*

Black Heathen, Octoroon, Quadroon, Mulatto, Red-bone, Yellow-Hammer, Paper-Sack
Brown I've been a Black American, a Negro twice, an Afro-American, a person of
African Decent

        An African American and an American with African Origins
        I've been 1/3 to 3/4 of whatever was politically correct
        When it's already been confirmed that
                "A Rose by Any Other Name Is Still a Rose"
From the Slave ships with Chains to the Selling Blocks with Whipping Post to the
Sugarcane and Cotton fields with Branding Irons
… And late night shame
… And Field hand Childbirths
…And Babies, MY Sweet, Tender BABIES TORN from my arms
        Oh God it's been so Hard Being Me!

I've been emancipated While being Hung and Degraded Been Torn to shreds with
water hose and Vicious Dogs For nothing, I tell you I was doing nothing , nothing more
than just marching, Marching for a Cause!

Cause I'm tired of being called E-V-E-R-Y THING
But a CHILD OF GOD…a child of God
 I TELL YOU!
 It's been so hard…SO Hard being me, just being me.
        So I Just Pray, I… Just…Pray!

"Wash Pot Tithing: A Family Legacy, The Family Tree"

Stories, which can be told as proverbs, rhymes, or narratives, are among the most powerful legacies we can receive from family because they provide morality and cautionary lessons to live our lives to their full potential. They are the chronological teachings of God's love, grace, and mercy. They teach the importance of family unity and determination. They declare the favor we receive when we learn from others' past life experiences, and warn us of the failures when we don't. By telling and re-telling these stories, whether factual or folklore, we pass our family histories on to generation after generation. We reflect on our consequences analogous to the old Negro spiritual, "How I Got Over." But whatever our ethnic or cultural origin, these stories are part of our family trees, embedded in our memories, planted as seeds to grow and flourish.

Our stories may be ministered from a gathering on a gallery (porch) at the end of the day, over the Sunday dinner table, at a family reunion, or after the funeral of a loved one. My mother periodically told the story of how she went to Wiley College. She recounted that story to people right up to the time of her death, and always became tearful when she told it. The moral of the story was not that she graduated, or the benefits of education, or even Wiley College's history, but of the loving act of family that allowed her the blessing and the benefit to attend.

In most family stories, the main character is a family member who sacrifices to see someone else's dream come to its fruition. Like so many students my mother met while she was in college, she was one of the first from her family to seek higher learning through the prayers and struggles of others. This act of love was rooted from John 13:34: "A new commandment I give to you, that you love one another; …" I always believed Jesus' act of unselfish love as He prepared to depart and be with the Heavenly Father was essential to receiving God's legacy and leaving ours. It was "the way," Jesus Christ's love and promise was handed down through the generations. 1 Corinthians 1:18 (KJV) says, "For the preaching of the cross is to them that perish foolishness; but unto us which are saved it is the power of God."

> "Nothing but the Blood
> This is all my hope and peace,
> Nothing but the blood of Jesus;
> this is all my righteousness,
> Nothing but the blood of Jesus."[55]

---

[55]"Nothing But the Blood" by Robert Lowery, 1876.

My mother's name was Annie Jean, and Ollie was her mother. The family set a goal of sending Annie Jean to Wiley College, and Geneva, Ollie's first cousin, was happy to do her part to make it happen. Geneva had been taking on extra work for about a year now. She was a wash woman, which some in the 1940s labeled "demeaning." It was the kind of service Negro women of that era were trying to liberate themselves from. But Geneva learned that to get to something better, she had to leave from something worse. One by one, prayer by prayer, and hard work by hard work, Geneva, "Gen" was moving her family from worse to better.

Gen was a practical woman, always thinking on her feet. In her early twenties she was already a maid, cook, and babysitter by profession, and a wife, mother, daughter, sister, niece, and cousin by inheritance. No one knew better than Gen that every position, whether vocational or by birthright, was a constant and demanding job. Gen never had a childhood; she inherited a sometimes absent father, an almost always ill mother, and baby brothers to take care of. She began learning the necessary duties to preserve her family at the tender age of five, duties that gave her the training to acquire the jobs she held now. Geneva symbolized her name, "woman" and "knee," by growing from a hard working praying girl into a hard working praying woman.

Gen did not mind the long hours or the hard work because of hard times; after all, she had been working hard her whole life. She learned to work in the fields when she was six or seven years old. Between the seasonal planting and harvesting work that surrounded the small northeast Texas town where Gen lived, she had little time for school. But Geneva never let that stop her from learning. She loved to learn and loved to read. It was a legacy she received from Aunt Lu, which is still being passed on.[56]

Family and town folks alike said Aunt Lu prayed and cried so hard over not being able to read that eventually someone could flip to any page in the Bible and she could read it, word for word. Now of course there will always be naysayers, like those who said Aunt Lu still could not read, but instead was reciting what she had heard over and over again. Either way, ain't God good?

"Nothing but the blood, nothing but the blood that saved me"

Anyway, Gen believed there was nothing wrong with an honest day's work for an honest day's pay, and she was proud of that attitude. On most days, she stopped at the market for her family, or one of the neighborhood's elderly, sick, or shut in. Then she entered the front door of her small wood-framed house, proceeded through the kitchen, and out her back door into her "little piece of peace"--her own back yard--where the big black wash pot was waiting for her. Next, she built a wood fire under the pot and sacrificed what she possessed: hard work, sweat, and love. Throughout her life, Gen also performed extra work for extra money to tithe to her church and into someone else's destiny.

---

[56] "I will instruct thee and teach thee…" (Psalm 32:8, KJV).

Most every day, Gen cheered her spirit and revived her mind and body by talking to the Lord and singing or humming a song. She learned early that when praises go up, blessings come down. She prayed simple and plain words like "Thank you, Lord, for helping me get this done, now, Jesus, help me down this road," and then she hummed and sang to herself.

Later when she recounted one particular day to the other women in the family, she said "I should have known something was about to happen." How many times had she heard and witnessed that "the Lord always sends a pebble (warning) before the devil throws a stone (trouble)?" The Holy Spirit was trying to tell her something but she had not been listening. She kept singing "Nothing but the Blood of Jesus" all day. When she got up that morning she was singing it, on the walk to work she was singing it, and all through the day she was singing it. No matter how she tried to change the tune, it kept coming back.

A lot of people, in their effort to be all they can be, want to erase the chapters of the history of their families they deem unacceptable or not dignified enough for the status they now hold or want to possess. It's as though they envision their ancestors being snatched off a throne in Africa and arriving in America setting up shop. Hello, Roots? But whether our forefathers and mothers arrived in America against their will as slaves, indentured servants, or seeking refuge from political or religious persecution or the great potato famine, ultimately they experienced insurmountable struggles. With each generation they pioneered forward so the next generation would have a better life. They took the little they had and built upon it. They were subjugated to harsh physical and psychological treatment, but by the grace of God and a plan, we, you, and I are here. We are America! I honor and give reverence to our elders, the sacrificial offerings of your family and mine, for it is their shoulders we stand on.

OK, back to the story. Like I was saying, no matter how Gen tried, she could not stop humming that tune. Well, this particular day seemed to be going according to Gen's plan. She finally got to the part of the day she set aside for the laundry; today it was Miz Amy's wash, including her "soiled rags."

At this point, the storyteller always interjects significant information to "keep it real," even though some may find it inappropriate: Although the first sanitary napkin was invented in 1895, it would be many, many years later before the napkins would be accessible for most women to purchase. In the meantime, women used homemade strips of folded old cloth (rags) to catch their menstrual blood, which is why the term rags was used to refer to menstruation. Some, like Miz Amy, had their homemade rags sewn together, washed with lye-soap to bleach and disinfect, and then lightly starched and ironed.

Gen was washing in the back yard when the devil started visiting with a hand full of stones. Through the baby crying, diaper changing, supper preparation, and old folks asking and re-asking the SAME questions, her little piece of peace was besieged with nosey neighbors, gossips, talebearers, and, to her dismay, the local drunk. That ol' devil was just throwing rocks every which way, now honey! Now, the local drunk just happened to be kinfolk, and absent of his wife, he had a "new" drunken floozy hanging all over him. Gen blocked the uninvited fools from her mind by humming to herself that same haunting song and thanking the good Lord for a good, hard working, God-fearing man.

Gen was a good listener. She learned early about men and marriage from the elderly women's gallery preaching, which always seemed to occur after some marital scandal. The evening preaching always began with Ms. Olna Mae calling the meeting to order with "I could write a book about men folk if I could spell all the words."

Aunt Laura always replied with, "If you can't be the bell cow, don't gallop in the gander" and "I wouldn't have a man who couldn't reach his hand in the cotton sack deeper than me."

Then Ms. Olna Mae would witness those words of insight with "Um hum Chile, just asking to live in hell while still on top of this earth; that's what that is. Honey, you ain't got to kilt me for me to learnt!"

Gen laughed to herself at the modern-day women who thought these old women's tag-team philosophy was outdated, ignorant, and too country, as if pretty city words meant you had common sense. These ol' head ragged warriors' words of life kept them and their marriages to a ripe old age. Gen was grateful to God she listened to Ms. Mattie and got her husband praying on her knees and not laying on her back.

> "Now by this I'll overcome
> Nothing but the blood of Jesus,
> Now by this I'll reach my home
> Nothing, but the blood of Jesus."[57]

This part of the story is where I always notice the tone of the storyteller's voice change, not to anger, but to tearful righteous indignation. Ephesians 4:26 says, "If ye have a just occasion to be angry at any time, see that it be without sin."

Mean-spirited folks live everywhere. Some people don't want to see us live better than they do, some people don't want us to do as well as they do, and some people just don't want to see us "do." They come with all forms of evil to hinder our progress. They will go out of their way with foolishness to try to instigate, agitate, or to humiliate the love right out of us.

Gen nearly finished the wash about the time all hell broke loose in her backyard. That ol' devil threw a brick right in the middle of her little piece of peace. It seems one of the nosey talebearers could not wait to run and tell kinfolk's crazy wife about Gen's cousin's new and improved

---

[57]"Nothing But the Blood" by Robert Lowery, 1876.

floozy. Why won't people mind their own business? Well, the brawl ended with kinfolk's wife knocking her drunken husband out, along with Gen's clothesline and the clothes. Then the wife finalized the country beat-down by wrapping the clothesline, clothes and all, around Miss Floozy's neck and dragging her through Gen's vegetable garden. She then dumped her husband's and Miss Floozy's battered bodies by Gen's blazing wash pot, sealing the deal with, "Now wash this filth or, better yet, burn it; they ain't nothing but trash anyhow."

Enough is enough, Gen thought. Her head, back, and legs ached, and her fingers and hands were rubbing-board sore. *If people can't mind their own business, why can't they just leave me alone?* Gen may not have had the power to cast those devils out of her uninvited visitors' bodies, but she did have the power to cast them off her property.

Time passed. Gen was not to be deterred. She was still thinking on her feet. As she re-washed the clothes and was ready to wring them out and re-hang back on the re-strung clothesline, she started softly humming to herself:

> "For my pardon this I see
> Nothing but the blood of Jesus
> For my cleansing this I see
> Nothing but the blood of Jesus"[58]

Geneva could see the end of a very long day on the near horizon. All she wanted was to take a bath, sit on her screened porch, and REST. At that moment she heard Miz Amy, with her blonde hair dripping with sweat and beet-red flustered face, frantically screaming Gen's name all the way from the road to the back yard. As she approached Gen, speaking with a plea but with eyes daring Gen to refuse, Miz Amy asked, "Geneva, dear, I know you probably had a full day, but I need you to wash these pads tonight and bring them with you in the morning. I know I may seem a little lazy…"

No, just low-down and downright nasty, Gen thought.

"…but I can't iron them as well as you.

With that spoken, before Gen could stop her, Miz Amy dropped a bloody bundle of dirty rags in the wash pot of sparkling white clothes. Upon seeing the distraught look on Gen's face, she said with a giggle, "Oh my! Maybe I should have given them to you. Oh well the well, as they say, 'It will all come out in the wash.'"As Miz Amy turned to walk away, she offered another demanding plea: "And, please, Geneva, remember very, very lightly starched."

As the boiling hot water and lye soap dissolved the dried blood of the rags and began to distort and discolor the pristine white of the wash, which had taken hours to achieve, all Gen could do was hum:

---

[58]"Nothing But the Blood" by Robert Lowery, 1876.

"Nothing can for sin atone,
Nothing but the blood of Jesus;
Naught of good that I have done,
Nothing but the blood of Jesus."[59]

Months later, Annie heard about that reprehensible day. She had returned from south Texas to visit her family in northeast Texas for the summer before going off to college. She loved Gen and knew Gen loved her. They were not only bonded by blood but by love and pain. This was an appreciation that kindled her soul; she would carry this indebted honor in her heart for family all her life. It was a debt that made them better, made them give more and love more. As fall approached, Gen sent word for Annie to come to her house as soon as she came home from work.

Gen planned to surprise Annie with money she had saved for her. As Gen stood over the wash pot, talking and thinking on her feet, she reached into her apron pocket and pulled out the money. In the blink of an eye a gush of wind lifted the money from Gen's hands and dashed it into the flames. Retrieving the money was to no avail. Instantly the hard-earned money was engulfed in the wash pot flames. This was the first time my mother had ever seen Gen break down into tears, and every time my mother told this story, right up to the time of her death, it brought her to tears, as well.

"This is all my hope and peace
Nothing but the blood of Jesus
This is all my righteousness
Nothing but the blood of Jesus"[60]

Annie put ointment on Gen's scorched hands and wiped Gen's tears that day, but it was Gen's words that would aid her and future generations. "Annie, you leaving for school. Remember, no matter what, you treat everybody right. Don't live in spite; we serve an all-seeing God. I don't know why we sometimes lose no matter how hard we try to win, perhaps because God is trying to tell us something and we so busy doing, we ain't listening. We sometimes get all caught up in our own plans and we forget it's not God's plans.[61] Now it's time to be a woman, not any woman, but a God–fearing woman. You got me and you got family; we got the same blood running through our veins. There's nothing stronger than that 'But the Blood of Jesus.'[62]

---

[59]"Nothing But the Blood" by Robert Lowery, 1876.

[60]"Nothing But the Blood" by Robert Lowery, 1876.

[61]"For I know the plans I have for you, declares the LORD, plans to prosper you and not to harm you, plans to give you hope and a future." (Jeremiah 29:11, NIV).

[62]"Nothing But the Blood" by Robert Lowery, 1876.

We washed, Annie; we nothing but filthy rags[63] washed in the blood of Jesus. Remember to always rejoice in your struggles 'cause baby, "To go to something better you have to leave from something worse."

"Glory! Glory! This I sing

Nothing but the blood of Jesus
All my praise for this I bring
Nothing but the blood of Jesus"[64]

The human blood that flows from woman produces life, and the human blood that flows within man retains life. But only through the blood of Jesus Christ does God give eternal life. In our daily walks, we, the children of God, are "Cleansed through the blood of Jesus," according to 1 John 1:7; redeemed through His blood, say Ephesians 1:7 and 1 Peter 1:18-19; justified by His blood, says Romans 5:9; receive peace through His Blood, according to Colossians 1:20; and are washed in His blood, according to Revelation 1:5. Never let your ambitions overshadow your anointing. It won't be what you do or what you are doing, but what gets done according to God's plan that will be of worth.

"Living On Our Grandmother's Prayers"

This morning the Holy Spirit blessed me with the memories of times I spent at my great-grandparents' home. Tears flowed down my face as I felt the incredible joy in knowing Jesus Christ as my Lord and Savior. I know Mama Annie Lee and Daddy Walker would be pleased that God heard their prayers and songs for generational blessings, which their children are still passing on. As I began to pray and praise the Heavenly Father for another brand new day, full of brand new mercies, the flow of praise began to move within me and I was carried back to those consecrated times.

I began to remember the annual summer visits to the country and those glorious Sundays of long yesteryears. I thought about how church mothers[65] of old rose early and showed all the virtues of the Proverbs 31 woman, and how these virtues were passed on, whether they were received or retained by every family member. Voices and sounds of the past called me from my bed and transported me back in time to the tinkering and scampering of hurried Sunday breakfast, accompanied by Mama Lee's singing in high spirits. All her children were under one roof, safe and happy. I began to sing with my great-grandmother's voice echoing in my ear, "If it wasn't for the Lord, tell me what would I do?"[66]

Her house always smelled of some delicious aroma broadcasting the after-church dinner menu, a carte du jour consisting of freshly baked corn breads, pies, cakes, and cobblers; southern-fried chicken and brown-sugared baked ham; purple-hull peas; turnip greens; corn on the cob; candied yams; macaroni and cheese; mashed potatoes and gravy; and, of course, rice. There was always an accompaniment of fresh garden vegetables. And no meal was complete without Mama Lee's famous tender hot-water cornbread and "sweet as a loving woman's heart" sweet tea. Every Sunday morning featured four generations of greats, grands, and parents rushing around and shouting orders to playful children: "Hurry up and get dressed! We're going to be late for church!"

---

[63]"But we are all as an unclean thing, and all our righteousness's are as filthy rags; and we all do fade as a leaf; and our iniquities, like the wind, have taken us away." (Isaiah 64:6 KJV)

[64]"Nothing But the Blood" by Robert Lowery, 1876.

[65]Story and its memories inspired by Pastor Eric Hancock's discussion, "Church Mother"

[66]Song, "He's Everything to Me," Anonymous.

As I reflected on those summer Sundays, the sweetest memories of the calmness and the peace that came over us as we bombarded the front door came to my spirit. Standing together in the doorway were my great-grandmother and my great-grandfather, smiling. Mama Lee was always dressed in her stewardess white and Daddy Walker, a quiet man of very few words but with a Godly heart of gold, in his steward black. They were husband and wife and prayer partners for more than sixty years. The memory of their love for each other and for us, the family, was so sweet and strong it brought the fragrances of Camay soap, Lily of the Valley, and Old Spice into the room.

I could feel my great-grandparents' love and God's presence, and I heard Mama Lee's prayer sing out from the past, still sealing our family's future. "If it wasn't for you, Lord, I don't know what we could have done. You, God, and you alone done brought us a mighty long way. And we want to thank you, Father, for this day you made and it is a blessing. You made it possible for me and Walker to see your love, mercy, and grace manifested in the faces, health, and prosperity of our children, Thank you, Lord! You've been water when we were thirsty and our food in barren lands. You brought comfort to us when we were sick. God, you been always there; God, you've been everything. Now, Father, as we gather into your house of prayer, let all receive your holy Word in the sermon. Give the parents the guidance on how to raise their children upright. And Father, bless these children with the obedience and the good common sense on how to act in church. Let them act like they've been raised properly with home training and manners, in correct and decent order, so that NO ONE gets a whipping this day...Amen."

Proverbs 13:22 says, "A good man leaveth an inheritance to his children's children: and the wealth of the sinner is laid up for the just."

"And so our mothers and grandmothers have, more often than not anonymously, handed on the creative spark, the seed of the flower they themselves never hoped to see--or like a sealed letter they could not plainly read."

---Alice Walker

"Recipe for the Holidays"

Stanza 1
I was feeling kind of melancholy, as holidays make me do
When I came up on a treasure of recipes,
a gift from them and now my gift to you
Big Mama's Gumbo boiling in a pot,
Aunt Alice's Sausage Gravy with Fluffy Biscuits to sopp
Mudear's Turkey and Dressing with trimmings to boot
Uncle Bill's home-made wine meant story telling time
which always caused a hoot
Someone always acted a fool; someone always said they'd shoot

Stanza 2
Aunt Hattie's Authentic Tamales when Mexico was really Mexico
Handed down from generation to generation
Or so the story goes
Mama Lee's Mustards and Turnips with Crackling Hot-Water Cornbread
Uncle Bud's How to Cook a Coon,
Miss Lizzie's Skillet Bread

Stanza 3
Billy and Troleon playing dominoes,
slammed the table so hard Mother's cake fell
Along with Aunt Toot's Self-Rising Rolls
Louise dancing in the middle of the floe, snapping her fingers, blues on the radio

Stanza 4
Miss Elgie's Chittlings,
Miss Tiba's Ham,
Miss Clydie's Sweet Potato Pie and Marshmallow yams
Cousin Gen's china all snowy and white,
A wash woman,
A maid
Who set a table of delight!

Stanza 5
I was feeling kind of melancholy
As holidays always make me do
When I came up on a treasure of recipes and memories
A gift from them
And now my gift to you

Our family history also includes the recipes and memories of cooking together, dining together, and laughing together. These simple times are treasured keepsakes of our past to be shared.

CHAPTER V

THE SUPERNATURAL CALL AND THE SUPERNATURAL SOUND

The word sound is both a transitive and intransitive verb, and it means to make a particular noise so as to be heard, or make something that produces such a noise. Sounds are the vibrations sensed by the ear. Such vibrations travel through air, water, or some other medium, and many are within the range of frequencies that can be perceived by the human ear. At sea level and freezing point, the speed of sound through the air is 1,220 km/760 mi per hour. This is a scientific definition, a common definition for a common sound.

But I am not talking about that kind of sound. When I speak of sound, I am talking about another sound, a supernatural sound. When I speak of sound, I am not talking about those who have forgotten the warnings of Matthew 6, who are seeking glory from men, or those who have forgotten the words of Ephesians 4: "I therefore, the prisoner of the Lord, beseech you that ye walk worthy of the vocation wherewith ye are called...." For they have forgotten and now speak unwholesome talk from their mouths, their words riddled with bitterness, rage and anger, brawling and slander, along with every form of malice. Theirs is a clamoring and carnal sound, a common sound from a common people. No...no, I am not talking about that kind of sound.

When I speak of sound I am talking about another sound, a supernatural sound. I am talking about a holy and anointed sound that can only be made by uncommon and "stayed on righteousness" people. This is the sound that activates God's manifestation and announces Him to all the earth with gladness. The uncommon people who make this kind of sound signal a joyful noise and cry out with gladness, for their pursuit and desire is to come and stay in the presence of the Lord. They know He is God, and they announce the truth because they are the sheep of His pasture. They enter His gates and courts with praise. They walk with Psalm 100 grafted into their being.

When these uncommon people open their mouths, a sound rises from their bellies and comes forth from their spirit, which results a ringing upon the land. They worship and serve a God who is good; His steadfast love has endured through the ages and through all generations of those who have and will come. They declare and decree a thing and it is so.

Prophetic poetry is that uncommon sound the Holy Spirit gives to the spirit man. He rises from the belly, comes forth out of the mouth, and His message is delivered through the poet's pen. Inspired by Apostle Theresa Harvard Johnson's, book Literary Evangelism beyond the Open Mic: Identifying Your Sound. Visionary Johnson is the founder and administrator of Voices of Christ Literary Ministries and the Scribal Anointing Literary Network.

The poem below is inspired by the teachings of Apostle Dr. Joseph B. Howard, Sr., the founder of Phoenix of Grace Ministries in Phoenix, Arizona. Apostle Howard is also a noted author and wrote the award-winning book, Battered Clergy, which was also made into a film. His message is for us to look at the tree and do better, to know our Bibles, our seasons, and our charges. "And he shall be like a tree planted by the rivers of water, that bringeth forth his fruit in his season; his leaf also shall not wither; and whatsoever he doeth shall prosper" (Psalm 1:3; Jeremiah 17:8, and 2 Timothy 2:1-26).

"Look to the Tree"

Stanza 1
There is a tree that grows by a living, flowing stream
Its service is humble yet its legacy is esteemed
It submits to order
From seed to sapling to tree
Its purpose is to fulfill its purpose to be a glorious tree

Stanza 2
Its roots are grounded
in earth's care

No burden
No canker worms
Only Godly prayers

Stanza 3
It stands noble in all seasons
Its trunk is hard and strong

Its leaves shade the heat of battle
Regardless of the weather
Regardless of the storm

Its branches a witness to the ages only bending to the Throne
Extend up to the heavens
Singing an angelic song "O Praise Him on High for He has done glorious things He is the Master of the lowly And the Master of the Kings"

Stanza 4

O be of good counsel! Look to the tree!

"Neither Fire, flood nor man's progression have been able to destroy me"

Drink from the living water, live your seasons, bear your fruits,

Consider the sovereign ordination of a royal root.

God is the Great I AM; He is Sovereign. Exodus 3:13-14 says, "And Moses said unto God, Behold, when I come unto the children of Israel, and shall say unto them, The God of your fathers hath sent me unto you; and they shall say to me, what is his name? What shall I say unto them? And God said unto Moses, I AM THAT I AM: and he said, Thus shalt thou say unto the children of Israel, I AM hath sent me unto you."

"Listen to the Wind"

Visitation and Counsel by the Holy Spirit
(The Narrator of this prophetic prose is the Holy Spirit speaking to the reader.)

Stanza 1
I AM HE and you are of ME; Bless His Holy Name
Hear MY Voice in the wind
Release and be born again[67]
Bless His Holy Name
What is in Heaven I brought to Earth
Listen to the wind

Stanza 2
Quiet Spirit…Broken Heart
Is the moment you become a part
of Supernatural liberty
Listen to the Wind
Your dusty sin is blown away; today you can be saved
Listen to the wind

Stanza 3
As simple as…The River becomes the sea
And a leaf is part of a tree
you can be an extension of ME
If only…
If only you will listen
Listen…listen…to the wind

Stanza 4
Every Creation on this Earth is within the Father's Birth[68]
Listen To the Wind
I AM HE and you are of ME
Release…Repent…Be Set Free[69]
Listen
When you pray
Listen…To…The…Wind

---

[67]"Being born again, not of corruptible seed…"1 Peter 1:23 (KJV).

[68]"Of his own will begat he us with the word of truth…." James 1:18 (KJV).

[69]Jesus answered, "Verily, verily, I say unto thee, except a man be born of water and of the Spirit, he cannot enter into the kingdom of God." John 3:5 (KJV)

When we pray we begin to enter into higher dimensions of His Holiness. As we grow in prophetic knowledge, receiving wisdom from our Heavenly Father we mature in our supernatural prayer life. The Holy Ghost will teach us to be still and to hear God. John 3:8 says, "The wind blows wherever it pleases. You hear its sound, but you cannot tell where it comes from or where it is going. So it is with everyone born of the Spirit."

"The Tapestries of Time"

Stanza 1

In my Father's house are many mansions
And in the mansions are many great halls
And within the great halls are mighty great walls
And upon these great walls are the tapestries of time

Upon each tapestry are intricate stitches upon stitches
DNA woven pictures that envelop time
Threads of human frailty entwined with a human hope,
Empowered by God's Glorious Riches
Strengthening our inner man
Canvases of indescribable colors
Exploding beyond imagination, reason, or rhyme
These are the foundations before the beginning of time.

Stanza 2

Weaved portraits depicting our purpose
Reveal the epitome of God's plan;
Our needle-pointed Genesis beginnings to the Revelations of our end.

Stanza 3

Gone are the dark hues of austerity and bleakness
Alleviated and poised through the origin of Ephesians 3
By the working of His omnipotent power,
God-Grace-Given-Love applied for you and me
We are the woven colors of inheritance purple and the richness of red-deeming blood.
We are saved by the Master's needle-pricked fingers
That dripped upon the tapestry, His Covered-Saving Love.

"Travailing in the Spirit"

Stanza 1

Push, Deliver, Bear Down, LET IT COME
Push, Deliver, Bear Down, ITS TIME HAS BEGUN
Push, Deliver, Bear Down, LET IT COME
Push, Deliver, Bear Down, CONTRACTIONS HAVE BEGUN
YOUR BIRTHING, YOUR GIFTING, YOUR SERVICE TO THE LORD

Stanza 2

Push, Deliver, Bear Down, Bow Down
TO RECEIVE GOD
The Water Has Broken, No abortion, long labor
No stillbirth, or caused fear
Submit to the Master
The crowning is near
Bear Down, Bow Down
Surrender to the throne

Stanza 3

Speak to it, Stand on it, March to it, FLOW THRU THE CORD
Speak to it, Stand on it, March to it, TRAVAIL TO THE LORD
Hear the Shofar,[70] Hear the Master; Hear the Son
Speak to it, Stand on it, March to it
THE BIRTHING HAS BEGUN

This poem was inspired by Psalm 139:13-14. You shaped me first inside, then out; you formed me in my mother's womb, and I thank you. Prophetess Anne Wright says on her CD, *Battle for Your Seed* (Genesis 1:1-31), "So God created man in his own image, in the image of God created he him; male and female created he them." Genesis 1:27 "So the Seed in me is the Word in me; and the Word in me is the God in me: and the God in me rises up every time I try to battle with the will of God. But because the Seed in me has overtaken the flesh, I have had to say God I give it up. I won't argue with You; I won't battle with You. I won't even try to figure You out, all I'll do is follow Your Word to the letter because if this is what it takes to receive 'the Anointing' I am willing to pay the price."

---

[70]A horn, usually a ram's horn, blown by the ancient Hebrews in battle and during religious ceremonies, now sounded in a synagogue on Rosh Hashanah.

CHAPTER VI

REBIRTHING FROM WOUNDED WOMBS: SUPERNATURAL CALL FROM SUPERNATURAL REVIVAL

"When I was a child, I spake as a child, I understood as a child, I thought as a child: but when I became a man, I put away childish things." --1 Corinthians 13:11(KJV)

As children we become familiar with such fairy tales as Cinderella, Sleeping Beauty, Snow White, and Beauty and the Beast. Though written for amusement, these fairy tales unlock a child's imagination in a positive way and encourage avid readers. In particular, the fairy tales I've named here have one common theme: "love conquers all."

These and other such stories also teach foundational principles and morals. Children learn that good overcomes evil and that reputable living is its greatest reward. These fables use imagination and creative visualization (affecting the outer world by changing people's thoughts and expectations; an on-switch to the human soul to live, love, and be loved) to bring rescue and love through a prince riding on a white horse.

One might ask, however, how fictional settings in a realistic world impinge on the child's ability to mature into a wholesome adult. Any child, whether female or male, who has not had a positive role model for validation, and thereby experiences feelings of abandonment, rejection, and loss of worth, may find solace and common ground with the characters and situations in such stories.

After all, many little girls grow up feeling unacceptable because they had no Godly father figure to love them, protect them, teach them how to live, and show them their worth. Likewise, many little boys who by natural instinct feel the need to defend and protect, grow up seeing themselves as inadequate in their manhood, not knowing what love is and how to love because of the absence of a Godly example of how to live.

Children who have lived such lives are more likely to exhibit low self-esteem as an adult, bent on a destructive path of constantly trying to prove they are worthy of love, admiration, and recognition. But imagine how different their outlook on life would be if their parents taught them about their Prince of Peace and Love through Biblical stories and scriptures written by the hand of God, instead of creative visualization stories written by mere men. 2 Timothy 3:16-17 says, "All scripture is given by inspiration of God, and is profitable for teaching, reproof, correction, and instruction in righteousness, that the man of God maybe perfect, thoroughly equipped to perform every good work." So, imagine how much more equipped they would be as living testimonies of good conquering evil if they knew their Heavenly Father and His love for them when confronted by the father of lies.

Every family has sayings that are instilled from generation to generation. "I can't stand a liar" was firmly taught, preached, and beaten into the children on the maternal side of my family. Few of us can hear those words and not recite verbatim, "'Cause if you lie you'll steal and if you'll steal you'll kill." Throughout my lifetime I have seen this word of correction and warning proven countless times. A lie is cancerous to the moral fibers of the soul and spirit. It is the rapist of holiness and Godly prosperity.

Proverbs 6:16-19 (KJV) says, "These six things doth the LORD hate: yea, seven are an abomination unto him: A proud look, a lying tongue, and hands that shed innocent blood, An heart that deviseth wicked imaginations, feet that be swift in running to mischief, A false witness that speaketh lies, and he that soweth discord among brethren."

"When Confronted by a Rapist"

When confronted by a Rapist

You'd better beware

Sometimes it's your soul that needs extra care

When confronted by a Rapist

Matters not its gender

Sometimes it's your spirit it seeks to hinder

Foul spirits come in a multitude of disguises

Flatterers, Plagiarists, Coveters, Thieves, Murderers, Liars

When confronted by a Rapist

Fear Not--Feed Not--Its insatiable lust

The Full Armor of God[70] will not tarnish--will not rust

When confronted by a Rapist

Hold tight your spirit's chastity key

The Key of David has been given to thee

(Isaiah 22:22; Revelation 3:7-13)

---

[70]Ephesians 6:10-17: "finally, my brethren, be strong in the Lord and in the power of His might. Put on the whole armor of God that you may be able to stand against the wiles of the devil…"

"Studying the Birth and the Afterbirth to Understand Rebirthing from Wounded Wombs"

Spiritual Birth, Part I

For purposes of this study, *birth* means the beginning of a natural or spiritual phenomenon. The terms *baby* and *infant* refer to the birth or manifestation of a gift or ministry. 1 Corinthians 11:8-9 and 11-12 say, "For man did not come from woman, but woman from man; neither was man created for woman, but woman for man.... In the Lord, however, woman is not independent of man, nor is man independent of woman. For as woman came from man, so also man is born of woman. But everything comes from God."

One of the most troubling and puzzling misfortunes affecting the ministry and the body of Christ today is the question of why our births--our gifts and our ministries--are not coming into existence. Even after long periods of being pregnant in the spirit and surviving excruciating labor and delivery, we are not seeing our Godly commissions come to fruition. We are not seeing the authenticity of our assignments being fulfilled. This two-part study approaches this subject using parallels between physical and spiritual labor and delivery.

The Delivery and Deliverance of Childbirth

The Middle Assyrians described a woman's difficulty in labor as a mother whose "door is blocked."[72] One Assyrian incantation recites, "The woman in travail has great difficulty in giving birth. She has great difficulty in giving birth; she is stuck with the baby..."[73]

The words *hard labor*, which come from the Hebrew word, *Qashah*, and refers to childbirth are used in 2 Kings 19:4, "This is a day of distress, of rebuke, and of disgrace children have come to birth, and there is no strength to bring them forth," and Genesis 35:16-20 (the account of Rachel's death in childbirth). Isaiah 13:8 ("And they shall be afraid: pangs and sorrows shall take hold of them; they shall be in pain as a woman that travaileth."(KJV)); Nahum 2:10 ("She is empty, desolate, and waste" (KJV)); and Micah 4:9-10 ("Now why do you cry aloud"(KJV)) refer to physical labor and delivery as an adversity.

A Parallel Observation

Any woman who has given birth knows the physical pain of contractions--the tightening of the muscles in the womb that occurs at increasingly frequent intervals, immediately before childbirth, that eventually push the baby out of the womb. Unfortunately, many expectant moms have been rushed to the birthing room only to be told "It's not time yet."

---

[72]Birth in Babylonia and the Bible, by Marten Stol and F. A. M. Wiggermann.

[73]Ibid.

Even after the long-awaited delivery, the mother has additional worries of whether she did all that was necessary to deliver a healthy infant, and whether she will be a responsible, good, and perfect mother. She wonders whether she will be strong enough and wise enough to protect her child from the misfortunes and evils of the world.

These same pangs suffered in the natural are also suffered in the spirit; it is the beginning of the birthing rite of passage. Unfortunately, somewhere along the way we forget who the Giver of the gift is and that all we have to do is heed, abide, and obey God for everything to work according to His perfect plan (Romans 8:28).

The Woman and the Dragon

Read Revelation 12:1-17. Quoting the points most important for this discussion, "And there appeared a great wonder in heaven…and the dragon stood before the woman who was about to give birth, so that when she bore her child he might devour it. She gave birth to a male child, one who is to rule all the nations with a rod of iron, but her child was caught up to God and to his throne…."
God placed the fleeing woman in the desert where she was cared for. A war in heaven between Michael and his angels, and the dragon (Satan) and his angels occurred. Satan and his angels lost the war and were hurled to the earth. Still pursing the woman, the dragon spews water from his mouth like a river to overtake the woman, but the earth opens its mouth and swallows the water.

Verse 17 says the dragon was enraged at the woman and went off to make war against the rest of her offspring--those who obey God's commandments and hold to the testimony of Jesus. I found profoundly interesting that both adversaries used their mouths and the river as weapons, the dragon for the destruction, and the earth for the safety of the woman. We, the "woman's offspring," can defeat the enemy with God's word from our mouths, according to John 7:38 and Isaiah 59:21.

Becoming a child of God is repentance. So go to work in God's vineyard. Bring forth the fruits of repentance that lead to growth.[74] "Our victory must come not through weeping or striving, but by faith that Jesus Christ has won the battle for us."[75] Romans 4:4-5 (KJV) says, "To him that worketh is the reward not reckoned of grace, but of debt. But to him that worketh not, but believeth on him that justified the ungodly, his faith is counted for righteousness."

---

[74] *Steps to Spiritual Maturity: How We "Grow" up in Christ,* by David E. Pratt.

[75] *Christ Has Won the Battle For You,* by David Wilkerson.

The Seed: The Word and the Beginning

Before we can effectively produce and prosper, we must have clarity of spiritual birthing, which begins with God and the seed. The seed is the multiplicity of God's wonder. The principles of seeds are quite simple with uniformity. *Beginning*, which means "origin," or "birth" is a synonym for seed, as in the book of Genesis, which starts with "in the beginning God created the heaven and the earth." Beginning with Genesis, the *seed* from plants, animals, and man multiplies throughout the Bible. The Bible itself is the beginning seed, for it gives light, truth, and victory.

Satan has direct hatred for the seed of woman. He finds delight in showing fault in the children of God and to delay, distract, and ultimately destroy our gifts, our divine purpose. Satan's sole function is to bring havoc, to abort and abolish God's decree upon our lives. But we can effectively produce, prosper, and be victorious over Satan when we have clarity of our spiritual birthing which begins with God and the seed.

Correlation, Activation, Revelation, and Manifestation

Correlation

The Enmity between the Seeds in Eden: Analyzing Genesis 3:15

Genesis 3:15 (KJV) says, "And I will put enmity between thee and the woman, and between thy seed and her seed; it shall bruise thy head, and thou shalt bruise his heel."

1   I (God--The creator of the universe)
2   Will (to command)
3   put (to place something)
4   Enmity (hostility)
5   Between (intermediate point; indicates choices of courses of action)
6   Thee (in this case Satan, the serpent)
7   Woman (female): the feminine pronoun, *she*, refers to the female or something traditionally known as female (e.g., nation, church).
8   Seed (source of the serpent)
9   Seed (children, descendants of the woman); beginning
10 It--used to refer to an object (enmity) or animal (Satan) and sometimes a baby (human)
11 Bruise (harm; cause injury)
12 Head (top part of body; center of intellect; crisis point; a critical juncture in a situation or series of events, at which time some action must be taken, however painful)
13 Heel (back of foot, an offensive term that deliberately insults somebody's, especially a man's, behavior)

The word enmity plainly means "hatred" or "hostility." The word it mentioned in number ten in the previous list is why it (Satan) wars against us (man) and we (man) war against it (Satan). But we have power over serpents and power to tread on them, according to Luke 10:19 and Romans 16:20. Paul writes of this enmity between the seeds in Ephesians 6:10-12 and warns us to stand against Satan's wiles. We fight against "principalities, against powers, against the rulers of the darkness of this age, against spiritual hosts of wickedness in the heavenly places." The Good News is while we are in the birthing room, we gain knowledge and wisdom for how to receive spiritual deliverance from spiritual warfare.

In pregnancy there will be two deliveries, one of the baby and one of the afterbirth. Spiritually, the term afterbirth means "remains," "residue relics," and "filtrates of past sins, character and generational flaws, hurts and betrayals." These contaminants pollute Godly destinies and create "wounded wombs." Only the scalpel of God's holy Word can totally heal these keloid-scarred wombs and make them whole without blemish and spotting. Hebrew 4:12 (KJV) says, "For the word of God is quick, and powerful, and sharper than any two-edged sword, piercing even to the dividing asunder of soul and spirit, and of the joints and marrow, and is a discerner of the thoughts and intents of the heart."

The Delivery of Spiritual Afterbirth, Part II[76]

Understanding the Correlation of Physical Afterbirth and Spiritual Afterbirth

The word *afterbirth* entered the English language in the 16th century, though is rarely mentioned in ancient texts. It derives from the Hebrew and Aramaic words *silja* and *siljta*, which consequently arrived at the Greek word *chorion*.

The afterbirth is the only disposable organ of the human body. Afterbirth is the combination of the placenta and the fetal membranes normally expelled from the uterus after the birth of the baby, hence, the word "afterbirth." The placenta is the organ that joins the mother and fetus (unborn offspring). It permits oxygen and nutrients to the fetus and facilitates the release of carbon dioxide and waste products from the fetus to the mother. Fetal membranes consist of the chorion, the outer membrane, and the amnion, the inner membrane that envelops the embryo and contains the amniotic fluid.

If the afterbirth is not expelled (delivered), the mother risks hemorrhaging and infection, which can cause permanent damage to the mother's reproductive system and result in terminal illness. An infant nursing from an infected mother will also become ill and potentially die.

---

[76]*The Amazing Placenta,* by Robin Else Weiss, LCCE.

Activation

The afterbirth serves the same function in both the physical and the spiritual birthing processes. In the physical, it serves as a shield protecting the placenta and fetus from attack by the mother's immune system. In the spiritual, it serves as a shield to protect and guard, to nourish and grow our spiritual development, to ensure a successful delivery of a thriving, God-given gift or ministry.

To be governed by the Spirit, we must live by the Spirit, and in the delivery of spiritual afterbirth, we must apply Romans 8 and Ephesians 6. Ephesians 6:12 (KJV) says, "For we wrestle not against flesh and blood, but against principalities, against powers, against the rulers of the darkness of this world, against spiritual wickedness in high places."

Revelation

Spiritual wounds are caused by generational curses,[77] which are the remainder of a deceased person's realm. Generations can pass on resentment, offenses, revenge, retaliation, self-destruction, and misguided traditional thinking and living. Just as a pregnant woman in the natural changes what she consumes in her body to retain health and not to pass on toxins to her unborn, the spiritually pregnant must also guard against contaminating spirits that invade the womb and devour our gifts and ministries before birth or in their infancies. These unteachable and unreachable spirits contaminate our spiritual health with arrogance, pride, fear, self-doubt, unbelief, unrepentance, and unforgiveness of past transgressions. And any gift or ministry suckling on a mother infected with these spiritual contaminants will become ill and die.

Like physical rebirth, spiritual afterbirth both repels and absorbs whatever we have taken in within our minds (thoughts and memories), and our hearts (feelings and emotions). It can either guard against or destroy our gift or ministry, depending on our choices. Christians functioning with remainders and reminders of past sins and hurts will act and react with behavior and characteristics deemed unholy, thus the term, *spiritual afterbirth*.

Hameyaledet [78]

The term *midwife* occurs in just ten explicit references to midwives in the scriptures, the principles of which have been passed on since Biblical times. Through God's directives, the spiritual midwife speaks commands to focus, thereby encouraging the emerging

---

[77] I was inspired by Apostle Marc Richardson to write about the residue of generational curses. Apostle Richardson is the founder and overseer of Kingdom City International and Prophetic Wind Ministries.

[78] "The childbirth assisting woman." For further reading, see "The Midwife to the Prophets," Apostle Adrienne Williams, by Prophetess Sandra Dukes. Apostle Williams is one of the God-assigned midwives and Pastor of the United Nations International Church in Jackson, Mississippi.. http://abcpreachers.ning.com/profiles/blogs/anointedworks-sd-presentsthe

prophets to bond with their prophetic spiritual gifts and come forth into their destinies.[79]

After the delivery, the midwife examines the afterbirth and determines if there is anything (chemicals, alcohol, DNA traits of abnormalities) within it that could potentially risk the baby's health or even its life. Likewise, the progression of birthing and delivery of healthy, holy gifts and ministries must be done in holy order, so as not to be birthed from wounded wombs filled with ungodly traits and unholy filtrates (See Psalms 22:9-10 and Proverbs 25:28). The only way we can accomplish this is to examine ourselves in light of God's Word. 1 Corinthians 11:27-32 (KJV) says, "...But let a man examine himself...For if we would judge ourselves, we should not be judged. But when we are judged, we are chastened of the Lord, that we should not be condemned with the world."

I was first introduced to the medical and spiritual comparison in a Bible study taught by Apostle Dennis Cook. So enlightened by his teaching, I began to research and study the subject further. God revealed to me that it's not enough to be healed but we must also let God's divine healing making us whole. (Mark: 1-40-42)The following chart details both physical and spiritual illnesses, their symptoms, characteristics, and results each type of sickness produces.

-----

[79] *Midwifery and The Bible Part I*: Genesis 35:16-18, by Beth and Larry Overton.

	Illness	Symptom	Characteristics / Effects	Results
Comparison Chart of Illness in the Medical -Physical – Spiritual Realm				
Medical	Flu	Low grade fever, sniffles	Aching body	Congested chest
		Coughing	High Grade Fever	Pneumonia
			Vomiting, Diarrhea	Collapsed lungs
				Death
Physical	Abused	Low self-esteem	Achiever-- Under/over	Promiscuous
	Victim	Insecure, anger, resentment	Unhealthy competitor	Unable to trust
			Approval seeker	Unable to recognize or give love
			Destructive and Self destructive behavior	Habitual lying
			Mental Illness	Alcohol, drugs Prison death
				Suicide

Comparison Chart of Illness in the Medical -Physical –Spiritual Realm continues				
Spiritual	Jezebel/Ahab Spirit	Control issue, Jealousy	Pride	Distrust
	Legion of Spirits		Power seeker/lust	Chaos
			Unhealthy competition	Breakdown of unity
			Mimicking	Suicide
			Manipulation	Stumped growth
				Death of ministry

Manifestation: Returning to God's Womb: An Act of Bravery

As an infant develops, grows, and matures in its mother's womb, so will those who return to the womb of God. Psalm 22:10 says, "I was cast upon thee from the womb." Rebirthing from a wounded womb is one of the most pure acts of bravery we will ever be called on to do: to recognize, accept, and then rid ourselves of those things we have become accustomed to, expected of ourselves, and have accepted into our nature and personality. One must dispose of the flesh in order to receive the Holy Spirit, who transforms us from a carnal being into a spiritual being with a renewed mind, a pure heart, and a righteous spirit powered by God.

Travailing through the spiritual birth canal, and transforming from carnal self to spiritual self to reunite with the Holy Spirit is not an easy delivery, for the yearning of the heart is not sufficient.

The only way we can be delivered healthy is to realign our spirits with the vision God planted in us with His Word. 1 Chronicles 29:17 says, "I know, my God, that you test the heart and are pleased with integrity. All these things have I given willingly and with honest intent." So be the noble contradiction that what the enemy meant for bad, God changes for your good. He changes miseries to ministries, terrors to testimonies, and resurrects sanctification out of sin and shame.

Conclusion

In Philippians 3:10, Paul reflects on his zeal for a deeper knowledge and relationship with Jesus and concludes: "I want to know Messiah and the power of His resurrection and the fellowship of His sufferings, becoming like Him in His death, and so somehow to attain to the resurrection from the dead. Not that I have already attained, or am already perfected, but I press on that I may lay hold of that for which Christ Jesus has also laid hold of me…"(Also see Philippians 3:7-14). The Father has said "If you will do these things acceptable to me then you may enter into the holiness of My Womb." (See Proverbs 2:1-22).

I thank God for His love, mercy, and kindness, for sending us all Cheerleaders for a Better World. It is my prayer that this book has inspired others to seek God more, love more, live more, and laugh more. God has created you and "you are beautifully and wonderfully made," says Psalm 139:14.

I hope by exposing myself and being transparent that these life experiences will lead someone to a more intimate relationship with God. Although my life is hid in Christ now, layers and layers of covers had to be removed before I found my true place in Him. My prayer is that each reader grows a stronger and more intimate relationship with God every day and that each reader learns, lives, laughs, and most of all, loves.

"You learn...So you plant your garden and decorate your own soul, instead of waiting for someone to bring you flowers. And you learn that you really can endure...That you really are strong and you really do have worth...And you learn and learn...
With every good-bye you learn."
--Jorge Luis Borges (Excerpt)

Sandra was once asked if she could give any gift to the world, what would it be? Sandra replied, "Compassion. If we become more tolerant and understanding of others, we would grasp that the great and Godly gift of charity is afforded to all who learn to love others as we love ourselves."

Sandra Dukes was born in Corpus Christi, Texas, to parents who put great emphasis on education and self-awareness. She was taught to be a woman of vision, to dream and believe in God and herself. She has two siblings, Roderick and Medina. Sandra's imagination was her primary playmate. She gives credit to these alone times as the beginning of her love to read and write poetry and stories.

In 28 years of work history, whether rushing down airline ramps or ripping up the fashion runways of Europe and stateside, Sandra always took time to appreciate the differences of others. Whether in the classroom or a conference room, as a student or teacher, Dukes observed that pure love and kindness is the universal key to opening locked doors. Whether doors of opportunity or hardened hearts, Sandra has learned that the holy Word and prayer are the rudimentary solutions to any situational or problematic circumstance. She has also learned that with God all things are possible.

She has learned in her life's journey that nothing will bring you more positive answers, joy, and peace than kneeling at the altar of grace where the Heavenly Father is seated. Prophetess Dukes now resides in Dallas, Texas.

Sandra Dukes is an ordained minister and has earned degrees, with influences in theater and literary arts. She holds diplomas and certificates in a wide range of career genres, such as her certificate from the Grigull Fashion Institute in Stuttgart, Germany. She is also a member of the International Toast Masters Club, Phi Theta Kappa and Delta Psi Omega Honor Societies, and the National Dean's List.

CONTACT THE AUTHOR

Anointed Works SD Ministries
9540 Garland Road Suite 381-335
Dallas, Texas 75218
(214) 997-3429
Email: anointedworkssd@yahoo.com
Websites: http://www.anointedworkssdukes.com
http://anointedworkssanctifieddestinies.ning.com/